A sweet surprise behind door number one...

Calista was about to close the door when she noticed someone else in the dark behind Karin. As he stepped toward the doorway, Calista's mouth fell open. The guy who arrived with Moa and Karin was tall and broad-shouldered. His brown hair was a little too long, falling in his eyes and curling around his ears. Even in the semidarkness, she could tell that his eyes were a deep, warm brown. He reached out to shake Calista's hand. She was relieved, since she seemed to have forgotten how to do anything but stand and stare. She finally remembered to close her mouth.

"*Hej!* My name is Håkan," he said. He smiled broadly at her. "Moa and Karin told me they were getting an American neighbor."

Calista's paralysis finally let go, and she smiled. "I'm Calista," she said, shaking his hand. "Did anyone ever tell you that you look like Prince Carl Philip?" *Oops, I can't believe I just said that,* she thought, using all her willpower not to fling her hands in front of her mouth.

"Is that a good thing?" Håkan asked, smiling. His smile was a little lopsided, as if they had a secret together.

"Ah, yeah, or, I mean," Calista blundered on. She'd be insulting him if she said no, and she would be giving him an embarrassingly huge compliment if she said yes. She shrugged her shoulders. "Oh, I don't know," she said vaguely. "I guess it depends on what you think of Carl Philip."

S.A.S.S.
STUDENTS ACROSS THE SEVEN SEAS

Swede Dreams

Eva Apelqvist

speak
An Imprint of Penguin Group (USA) Inc.

SPEAK
Published by the Penguin Group
Penguin Group (USA) Inc.,
345 Hudson Street, New York, New York 10014, U.S.A.
Penguin Group (Canada), 90 Eglinton Avenue East, Suite 700, Toronto, Ontario, Canada M4P 2Y3
(a division of Pearson Penguin Canada Inc.)
Penguin Books Ltd, 80 Strand, London WC2R 0RL, England
Penguin Ireland, 25 St Stephen's Green, Dublin 2, Ireland
(a division of Penguin Books Ltd)
Penguin Group (Australia), 250 Camberwell Road, Camberwell, Victoria 3124, Australia
(a division of Pearson Australia Group Pty Ltd)
Penguin Books India Pvt Ltd, 11 Community Centre, Panchsheel Park,
New Delhi - 110 017, India
Penguin Group (NZ), Cnr Airborne and Rosedale Roads, Albany, Auckland 1310, New Zealand
(a division of Pearson New Zealand Ltd)
Penguin Books (South Africa) (Pty) Ltd, 24 Sturdee Avenue, Rosebank, Johannesburg 2196,
South Africa

Registered Offices: Penguin Books Ltd, 80 Strand, London WC2R 0RL, England

Published by Speak, an imprint of Penguin Group (USA) Inc., 2007

1 3 5 7 9 10 8 6 4 2

Copyright © Eva Apelqvist, 2007
All rights reserved
Interior art and design by Jeanine Henderson. Text set in Imago Book.

LIBRARY OF CONGRESS CATALOGING-IN-PUBLICATION DATA
Apelqvist, Eva.
Swede dreams / by Eva Apelqvist.
p.   cm.—(S.A.S.S.: Students Across the Seven Seas)
Summary: In order to get away from her annoying twin sister, and to be with her
boyfriend who was a Swedish exchange student at her Wisconsin school, sixteen-year-old
Calista spends a semester in Sweden, where she learns about more
than just the language and culture of this Scandinavian country.
ISBN: 978-0-14-240746-2 (pbk.)
[1. Study abroad—Fiction. 2. Schools—Fiction. 3. Interpersonal relations—Fiction.
4. Identity—Fiction. 5. Sweden—Fiction.]
I. Title. II. Series.
PZ7.A6364 St 2007
[Fic]—dc22   2006044359

SPEAK ISBN 978-0-14-240746-2

Printed in the United States of America

This book is dedicated, with my deepest gratitude, to my wonderful host family—Jim and Judy Olson, Ellen Wermuth, Diana Holmquest, and Jennifer Dolan.

Calista's Stockholm

Klara Norra Gymnasium

Historical Museum

Gallerian

National Museum

Skansen

Gamla Stan

Grödinge

Application for the Students Across the Seven Seas
Study Abroad Program

Name: Calista Swanson
Age: 16
High School: Moon Lake High
Hometown: Moon Lake, Wisconsin
Preferred Study Abroad Destination: Stockholm, Sweden

1. Why are you interested in traveling abroad next year?

Answer: I have always been interested in other cultures and languages, but because of my parents' business—custom-made pottery for our retail store and other companies—we can't travel. A friend introduced me to the Swedish culture and language, and I have been taking Internet classes on the Swedish language ever since. Now I want to take my language learning one step further by attending classes in a Swedish high school.

(Truth: I want to hook up with my Swedish boyfriend, Jonas, who was an exchange student at our high school in Wisconsin [though the stuff about learning Swedish is actually true, too—I love that funny sing-song language].)

2. How will studying abroad further develop your talents and interests?

I hope that by experiencing another culture, I will learn new things about our American culture as well. I hope to use this knowledge when making career choices later on.

(Truth: I have lots of interests but not a lot of talent. My twin sister, Suzanne, was bestowed with all the talent in our family.)

3. Describe your extracurricular activities.

Answer: Student council, yearbook staff, sports reporter for the student newspaper

(Truth: I don't have time for anything other than glazing and firing my parents' pottery, and working the gift shop and the coffee counter. If you don't have any talents, you have to serve those who do.)

4. Is there anything else you feel we should know about you?

Answer: I am a curious, outgoing person who loves meeting new people and learning new things.

(Truth: Hey, that _is_ the truth.)

Chapter One

"Cal! What did you do?" a voice said from the doorway.

Calista took a few dancing steps in the middle of the messy bathroom, trampling the carpet of black hair around her feet. She set the scissors in the sink and fluffed her now much shorter hair. "Like it?"

Calista's twin sister, Suzanne, moved her hands to her own hair, which was still in a bun from playing the piano at church that morning. "We look…different now," she said.

Calista couldn't tell from her voice if this was a good thing.

"You did a nice job, though," Suzanne added quickly. "You've always been good at that sort of thing."

Calista stopped and turned to face Suzanne. "What sort of thing? Playing with scissors?"

Suzanne sighed. "I don't know…fashion improvements."

"Fashion improvements, Suze? How did you guess that's what I always wanted to be famous for?" Calista said sarcastically, and shook her head.

"Cal, why do you take everything I say the wrong way? You're good at lots of things."

"Mm-hmm, right." Calista grimaced, cleaning the scissors in the sink. "Don't even go there, Suze," she said. They both knew Suzanne was the one with talent in the family. She was the gifted piano player, the gifted potter, soon to be the gifted Juilliard School of Music student.

Calista sighed and put the scissors back in the cabinet. There was something about being around Suzanne that made her so irritated she could hardly stand herself. But she didn't want her irritation to ruin her last evening at home. She lifted her eyes to the mirror, cocked her head, and looked at her new self. Suzanne was right. Though the twins were both tall, thin, and dark, like their mother, they didn't look alike anymore. Good! She liked her new look. Her thick, wavy, shoulder-length hair and bangs emphasized her high cheekbones and her large brown eyes. Suzanne's stiff bun looked drab in comparison.

"This hairstyle makes me feel kind of…metropolitan," she said with a sweep of her arm, trying to brush away the tension between them. "Do you think Jonas will like it?"

Suzanne shrugged. "You should have donated your hair to Locks of Love."

Calista laughed. "I checked. They want locks, not sticks, and it has to be ten inches long. This is only about five. So do you think Jonas will like it?" she asked again.

Suzanne sat down on the toilet lid. She still didn't answer Calista's question.

Calista decided to ignore her. She swept the hair from the floor and dumped it in the trash, humming "Jingle Bells" rather loudly. Okay, so Suzanne wouldn't talk about Jonas. See if she cared. Suzanne was just jealous of the attention Calista got when she started going out with Jonas.

Suzanne sighed again and left the bathroom. Calista's obnoxious post-Christmas humming had obviously served its purpose.

When she finished cleaning up in the bathroom a few minutes later, Calista followed Suzanne into the kitchen for supper.

"Nice hair, honey," Calista's dad called from the kitchen sink. He was scrubbing clay from his elbows. In the blinking red Christmas lights from the kitchen window he looked like a dusty Santa Claus with his bushy white beard.

"Thanks," Calista said. She tugged playfully at his beard. "Christmas is over, Dad, time to shave."

"Hey," her dad said. "I get to keep it until New Year's. That's the tradition."

Calista looked at her mom, her eyebrows raised.

"He's right," her mom said, nodding. She was scraping something into the compost bin underneath the sink. "The rule is October 1 to January 1." She turned to look at Calista. "Very nice haircut, Cal," she said.

"Thanks, Mom." Calista leaned over the roasting pan that was cooling on the stove, breathing in deeply. She loved the homey smell of turkey.

"Say, Suzanne," their dad called. Suzanne was at the table, picking pieces of red bell pepper from the salad bowl with her fingers. "Father Lucas was talking about you after Christmas services yesterday. He said his mother goes to church just to hear you play the piano." Dad chuckled. "I didn't tell him that's the only reason I go as well."

Calista pulled out her chair. "Could you please use your fork," she said in Suzanne's direction. "Hey, I get to see Jonas in less than twenty-four hours," she said to everyone.

Their dad was grinning now, still scrubbing away at the clay. "Yeah, how fun. You'll have to say hi to that soccer player of yours." At least someone in the family was willing to talk about Jonas. "That guy scored more goals than Moon Lake has seen in a single season since—"

"—we started the soccer league ten years ago," Suzanne interrupted in a bored voice. "We know, Dad."

Dad didn't seem to notice Suzanne's sarcasm. "He's a keeper, Cal!"

"I intend to keep him," Calista said, smiling. She might not play the piano, but at least she was good at something, she thought, like choosing boyfriends her dad approved of.

Still, Jonas was the best. He and Dad had really hit it off, going over offside rules, out-of-play balls, and fouls like they were already family. It did complicate things that Jonas was only an exchange student and that he lived in Sweden. Though secretly, for Calista, that was part of the attraction. Dating a Swede would help her add another foreign language to her small collection of Spanish and French.

In fifth grade, when she first took French, it was as though a secret world opened up to her. A few years later she discovered that Spanish held yet another world. It was as though with a different way of saying things came a whole new way of thinking—new music, new literature, new ways to look at life, new everything. How could she resist when adorable Jonas had offered to help her learn Swedish?

"He's a nice guy, don't get me wrong," Mom interrupted Calista's thoughts, "but surely, Bill, there are better reasons for choosing a boyfriend than the fact that he's an athlete. If I would have picked that way, I would never have found you."

"Really?" Dad said with mock seriousness. "You mean you didn't marry me because I never missed a Packers game in my entire life?"

Cal and her parents laughed, but Suzanne remained quiet.

"I wonder when I'll eat turkey next," Calista said, changing the subject as she speared a piece of turkey with her fork. The yummy dark meat, surrounded by mashed potatoes slathered in gravy, was her favorite meal. "From now on, it'll be Swedish meatballs and *smörgåsbord* 'til kingdom come."

After dinner, Calista checked her e-mail, hoping for a message from Jonas. Maybe he had finally gotten back from wherever he had gone for Christmas, since he clearly wasn't home. But no, there was just that same old e-mail from almost a month ago sitting in her in-box. She knew it by heart.

To: Calista@email.com
From: JonasVonC@email.com
Subject: Soon

Calista, Cal, Callie,

I miss you. There are a ton of places I want to show you in Stockholm. Let me know when you're coming. I lost your other e-mail.

I thought when we talked you said you were coming for a visit. But you'll be here for a whole semester??? And you're staying with a Swedish family?

Anyway, there's this tower, Kaknästornet, on Gärdet. It's one of the tallest buildings in Stockholm, and they have a spinning restaurant at the top. I can't wait to take you there. It's like being on top of the world. You can see the whole city. That'll be a cool place for us to watch the fireworks on New Year's Eve.

Jonas

Even if he was bad about getting back to her, it was good to know that Jonas would be there to guide her around Stockholm—and to practice Swedish with. But why didn't he remember when she was arriving? It's not like she hadn't told him. They had talked about it many times. But it wasn't that important, she reasoned. She could call him from her host family's house when she got there.

Calista turned the computer off and raked her hands through her shorter hair. Even though she had cut only about five inches, it felt funny. What if Jonas *didn't* like it? Of course he would, she decided, absentmindedly picking the needles off the tiny Christmas tree on her desk. Then her thoughts shifted. She was leaving tomorrow morning. Was she ready to go? Where was her passport? Had she packed her tickets? Oh, and the Swedish dictionary, she needed that in her carry-on so she could practice on the

plane. Jonas had taught her a few words and phrases, and she had taken an Internet class, but she was set on learning Swedish faster than anyone in history. She had already discovered words for which there were no synonyms in the English language, like *ombudsman* and *smörgåsbord.* They were even used in America.

She rummaged through her carry-on backpack to make sure the dictionary was there. Everything seemed to be in place, including the good-bye and good luck and don't-forget-us card from her best friends, Sammie and Leah, which she had promised to keep on her desk in Sweden.

By this time tomorrow she would be on the other side of the Atlantic Ocean, she thought as she climbed into bed. She tried taking a deep breath, but it wasn't until she reminded herself that Jonas would be there, on the other side, that she could relax and…oh no, not the piano. Calista looked at her clock. She got up, opened her door, and went to the top of the stairs.

"Suzanne!" she called, the irritation obvious in her voice.

The playing stopped. "What?"

"Do you know what time it is?"

"Ten thirty."

Unbelievable. She had to spell out everything. "Could you please not play right now? I'd like to get some sleep before tomorrow."

Calista turned, satisfied, and went back into her room.

A few seconds later, she heard footsteps stomping up the stairs. Her door opened, and Suzanne stood in the doorway.

"Why do you think you're the only person who matters here, Cal?" Suzanne said. "When Calista Swanson goes to Sweden, everyone in the entire world should freeze their lives and tiptoe around her—"

"It's ten thirty," Calista said. She so didn't want to argue. She turned and got back into bed. She just wanted to get some sleep.

"Like you're not usually on the phone with Leah or Sammie until past midnight," Suzanne said.

Calista pulled her pillow over her head, trying to will her sister away. Eventually it worked. She heard the door closing behind Suzanne, a little too hard, and then her not-too-quiet feet on the stairs. At least this made it easier to leave. She would not miss Suzanne and her piano. She couldn't wait to get to Sweden.

Calista's ears ached from the steep ascent and the change in air pressure. The parking lot was shrinking below the airplane window. Through the falling snow she could see the cars growing smaller. One of those tiny tin cans was her family's red Geo Prizm, she thought. In it, her mom and dad and Suzanne would be driving the two hours from the Minneapolis airport back home to Moon Lake, Wisconsin. They would barely have time to park in front of their white

Victorian house before Mom and Dad would hop out and hurry to the pottery studio next door to start preparing for classes the following day. Suzanne, of course, would practically run to her piano to practice for hours, getting ready for her audition for the Juilliard School of Music admissions committee in early March. And for once, Calista wouldn't have to be there to listen.

There was no place she would rather be than on her way to Sweden, where she would spend an entire semester gallivanting around Stockholm with Jonas. She would learn to speak Swedish like a native, and, best of all, she wouldn't have to hear the incessant harping about the wonderful talents of Queen Suzanne.

Calista popped a piece of spearmint gum into her mouth and chewed hard, trying to get her ears to pop. She turned to the pale blond girl sitting next to her in the aisle seat and held out a stick.

"Hey," she said, trying to get the girl's attention. "Want some gum?"

Not looking at Calista, the girl, who appeared to be Calista's age, shook her head vehemently, her eyes glued on the flight attendants moving up and down the aisle. Her shoulders were pulled up to her ears, and her hands were trembling. A magazine fell from her lap. Since the girl didn't seem to notice, Calista bent to pick it up for her. *FiberARTS*. A puppet made entirely from white buttons adorned the cover, which promised articles about digital quilting, new fiber collage techniques, and tactile interpretations of life. This magazine was clearly up there with *Car and Driver* and *Modern Woodworking* on the excitement index.

"You like sewing?" Calista asked. "My sister sews." And plays the piano, and cooks gourmet meals, and creates pottery, she thought with an involuntary shiver.

The girl, who was breathing rapidly, kept watching the flight attendants. When Calista received no answer, she stuck the magazine in the back pocket of the seat in front of the girl and turned to the movie screen above her head. An overly friendly woman was demonstrating how to blow up a life jacket should the plane miraculously land smoothly on the surface of a large body of water, and should the people on the plane still happen to be alive after a drop of a few thousand feet. The scenario was enough to give anyone an anxiety attack—not good entertainment for panic girl. To the rescue…

"Going to Sweden or Iceland?" Calista asked, turning to the girl.

The girl kept her eyes on the video, the one *she should not be watching.*

Calista changed tactics. "Do you know you're more likely to get hit by a meteorite on the ground than have your airplane fall out of the sky?" she said.

Finally, she had the girl's attention. Looking far from

convinced of the meteorite statistic, she turned to Calista, her blue eyes wide open. "Is it that obvious?" she said in a Swedish accent.

Calista nodded. "Yup."

The seat-belt sign went off above them. "I have to use the restroom," the girl said.

Calista nodded, and after the girl disappeared down the aisle, she closed her eyes, allowing herself to daydream—it was finally happening. She had waited six months for this day to come, ever since Jonas left Moon Lake in June.

Soon, she'd be strolling hand in hand with him through Stockholm's snow-covered winter streets, chatting happily in Swedish, drinking espressos in cozy cafés, shopping for trendy clothes in exclusive department stores. She conjured up Jonas's serious freckled face and blond hair, his smell of aftershave, his deep voice with a Swedish accent. She couldn't wait to see him in action on the soccer field again—Dad had made her promise to report on Jonas's soccer games—though that would probably have to wait until spring since he didn't play in the winter.

The plane jumped. Calista smiled and pulled herself out of her dream cloud to retrieve her Swedish phrase book from her backpack. She flipped through a few pages until she started thinking about her host parents, Bengt and Britta Öhström.

Bengt was a preschool teacher, and Britta was a computer programmer for Vattenfall, the state-owned energy company. On their application form they said they wanted a student who would do things with the family. She wasn't sure how much time she'd have for them. Then again, even though she wanted to see Jonas, she also wanted to do family things. Besides, Bengt and Britta would probably love Jonas—how could they not?—and they wouldn't mind having him along whenever they spent time together.

Calista thought about the study abroad application *she* had filled out. Maybe she should have mentioned Jonas....

The pale girl returned, looking somewhat more relaxed. She almost smiled at Calista as she sat down. Then, for a nanosecond, the plane dropped straight down. A collective gasp went through the cabin, and the girl let out a moan, her pale face taking on a tinge of green. Her eyes closed, and she gripped the armrests of her seat so tightly her knuckles turned white.

"It's only an air pocket," Calista said, putting as much cheer into her voice as she could muster.

The girl opened her eyes. "What did you say?" she whispered hoarsely.

"I said it's only an air pocket."

Again, the plane dropped, then shook violently. The girl's eyes were huge. She moved one white-knuckled fist from her armrest and covered Calista's hand with her own.

"Are they normal?" she asked, tears welling up in her eyes.

Calista tried not to react to the pain of the girl's nails digging into her flesh. She nodded and smiled. "Yeah, they're nothing. Don't worry. Look at the flight attendants. They're still serving drinks. Is this your first flight?"

The girl, her eyes flitting between Calista and the flight attendants, looked like she was going to nod, then she caught herself. "My second. My first was going the other way. I visited my cousin in Minneapolis, and now I'm going home."

Calista smiled. "Your English is great," she said. "That's how good my Swedish will be in three weeks....Not."

Now the girl did smile. She noticed her hand on Calista's, blushed, and removed it. "I love your hair," she said.

"Thanks."

"By the way, I'm Lena," the girl said. "When I flew to Minneapolis, I tried thinking of things I hate more than flying, like having a root canal. It didn't work. All I could think was: Anything is better than this."

Calista laughed. "Calista," she said. "Or Cal."

"You must be a fast learner if you're going to pick up Swedish in three weeks," Lena said. "Or do you already know some?"

"*Lite grann*," Calista said, showing a half-inch space

between her thumb and her index finger. "With emphasis on *little*. My boyfriend, Jonas, taught me."

"Is he Swedish?"

Calista nodded. "He was an exchange student at my school. After I got to know him I took an Internet class in Swedish. Swedish is such a pretty language. Then I applied and was accepted to the S.A.S.S. program to come to Sweden. I'm not good at speaking yet, but I'll be going to a regular high school, I mean *gymnasium*, and all my classes will be in Swedish. If I don't pick it up quickly, I'm history. School starts the second of January, in less than a week."

Lena nodded. "Mine, too. And I switched schools this year, so it'll be scary for me also. So what about this boyfriend?"

"What about him?"

"Well…what's he like?"

"Oh, he's, um, a great soccer player. And he's good-looking, and…I don't know…popular, cute, well dressed…"

She pulled Jonas's picture from her wallet.

Lena put the picture close to her face, cocked her head as though contemplating a work of art, then nodded and smiled.

Lena had a nice face. It was easier to tell now that she didn't look petrified. The corners of her mouth curled up even when she wasn't smiling, and she had a tiny gap between her front teeth.

"Cool necklace," Calista said after a minute. Lena's necklace was made from multicolored yarn in earthy tones of brown and green. A number of strings had been bundled together into a thick cord, and on the individual strings, tiny glass beads were attached in an irregular pattern. "It makes me think of a forest."

"Thank you," Lena said. "That's a nice compliment. Now if you'll only talk to me nonstop until we land in Iceland in six hours or so, I'll be fine. You might as well put that phrase book away. I won't leave you alone for a second."

They both laughed.

"I told you about Jonas," Calista said, leaning back in her seat. "Tell me about your boyfriend."

Lena chuckled. "What makes you think I have a boyfriend? Does everyone you know have one?"

Calista wrinkled her brow. Suzanne didn't have a boyfriend. She might be good at everything else, but she didn't attract cute, athletic guys the way Calista did. Leah and Sammie didn't have boyfriends either, come to think of it. "Okay, good point," she admitted.

"My guy stories are so not interesting," Lena said. "I'll tell you about some things you shouldn't miss while in Sweden, though."

After six hours of nonstop talking; a change of planes in Reykjavik, Iceland; then another three-hour flight, during which she was sadly not seated next to Lena but beside a businessman who snored so loudly she felt like pouring her cup of ice water over him, and Calista finally stumbled off the plane in Stockholm. She'd been awake for much too long and was beginning to feel like she was moving around underwater—every step was slow and heavy.

Calista saw and promptly lost Lena again in immigration, where Lena walked right through and Calista had to stop and show her passport and student visa. Then she followed the stream of Iceland arrivals to the luggage retrieval area. People all around her were talking on their cell phones. She wouldn't call Jonas today, though, she thought. It would be polite to give her host parents her undivided attention the first day. Besides, it would give her a chance to sleep away the dark circles under her eyes.

Calista grabbed her large black suitcase from the carousel and proceeded through the customs checkpoint until she found herself moving into a large arrival hall in the middle of which stood an enormous Christmas tree sparkling with tiny white lights.

Calista stopped in her tracks, gazing at the tree. She took a deep breath, inhaling the smell of cinnamon buns from the coffee shop across the hall. She turned her head slightly to the left and... he *did* remember!

Chapter Two

Jonas had his back to Calista. She started walking toward him. His hair was short, shorter than she'd ever seen it, and he had a different winter coat from last year. He must not have noticed that her plane had landed. She ran the last few steps and threw her hands over his eyes from behind.

"Guess who?" she called.

Before she could blink, the young man spun around, looking at her with nostrils flared and a wild expression in his eyes. He wasn't a day over thirteen.

"Oh, God," Calista said, blushing. "I'm so sorry. I thought you were someone else."

"It's okay," the boy stammered, politely addressing her in English while carefully edging backward, away from her.

Darn, Calista thought, blushing fiercely when she noticed the boy had crossed the room and was pointing her out to his family. Of course he wasn't Jonas. How could she have been so stupid? Jonas couldn't even remember what day she was arriving.

Calista pushed her embarrassment aside to take in her surroundings. All around her, people were waiting. Cabdrivers were standing in a semicircle and holding large poster boards. PÅL ANDERSSON one said, JOHAN KRUSE another. A blond family with three children was waving flowers and balloons, and the mother, presumably, held a sign that said VÄLKOMMEN HEM SARA!

Calista, having moved on from her attack on the innocent kid, grinned and twirled around, trying to capture everything in front of her.

The outside walls of the arrival hall were made of glass, and through them, in the dusk, Calista could see taxicabs and police cars, and people with luggage carts—the same sights one would see in the Minneapolis airport. Tiny snowflakes were falling, just like in Minneapolis, and disappearing as soon as they touched the ground. Only, this wasn't Minneapolis or Wisconsin, she reminded herself. It was Stockholm, and all around her, people were speaking Swedish, much too quickly for her to pick up even a single word.

Calista's eyes returned to the inside of the hall. Most of the people around her looked stylish. It was painfully clear that not one had gotten her hair cut at Davidson's Barber in Moon Lake, or at the Calista Swanson Salon for that matter.

"Hey, Calista! Thanks for helping me keep calm on the plane."

Calista turned and smiled at Lena and a woman who, judging from her blond hair, long thin legs, and pale skin, must be Lena's mom. The two of them looked like a pair of models, á la Scandinavia. Calista gave Lena a quick hug before taking the hand the blond woman held out.

"I'm Pia Warrén," she said.

"Calista Swanson," Calista said. "Nice to meet you."

"You, too. From the arrival area to here I've already heard lots about you. I hope you'll be coming over to visit soon. Lena must have told you that we don't live too far from your host family."

"She did. I would love to visit. I'll e-mail you, Lena," Calista said, "and we can get together after school starts."

Lena and Calista traded e-mail addresses, and then Lena and her mother said good-bye and disappeared out the sliding-glass doors.

She was alone no more than a minute before she heard, "Calista?"

Calista turned to the voice next to her. There was no mistaking this man—Bengt! He looked just like he did in the picture attached to the host-family information form—big nose, big glasses, hair like Einstein, gangly arms and legs like an overgrown calf. He had a wide grin on his face.

Bengt scooped Calista up in his arms as though she were a long-lost relative. Calista gasped for air. Where were all those shy Swedes she'd read about in her guidebooks?

"Hi," she managed when he finally let go of her. "I mean, *Hej.*"

"Your hair is shorter," Bengt said. "Nice."

Calista nodded, blushing, "Yeah, it's short now. But it was long in the picture I sent you." Oh, that was brilliant. She hoped she wouldn't be called upon to have any more profound conversations today. She turned toward the short, dark woman who had joined them and was now extending a hand to her. "You must be Britta," Calista said, shaking her hand. Britta looked like a rock, solid and strong, though probably a foot shorter than Calista.

"We are so happy to have you with us, Calista," Britta said, smiling widely. "We can't wait to show you Stockholm."

Bengt lifted Calista's suitcase. "Let's get going," he said. He carried the suitcase as though it were no heavier

than a matchbox, talking nonstop as they walked, mixing Swedish and English in a way that was unbelievably confusing to Calista's jet-lagged brain.

Britta must have noticed Calista's weary expression. "There's no off button, I'm afraid," she whispered, grinning.

"Hey, I heard that," Bengt called from up ahead. Calista smiled and looked around. Other than the signs being in Swedish, this airport could have been anywhere in the world—anywhere it snowed, that is.

Bengt led them into the underground parking lot. It was full of tiny, compact cars. There was not one truck or van or even a minivan as far as Calista could see. Actually, it would have been impossible to park anything but a tiny car in those parking slots.

Bengt popped the trunk of a blue Toyota.

"Cute car," Calista said. "I've heard that they get something like forty miles to the gallon. My mom is into environmental stuff."

Bengt smiled. "Hmm, now I'll have to use my head," he said. "How many kilometers per liter is forty miles per gallon?"

"Seventeen," Britta said quickly.

Calista's mouth dropped open. "Get out of here!" she said. "How did you do that?"

"Oh." Britta laughed. "It's a bad habit I have, calculating everything in my head, trying to beat Bengt."

"She's set low standards for herself," Bengt said good-naturedly.

As Britta drove the Toyota away from Arlanda Airport, heading south toward the city of Stockholm, Calista watched the white Swedish landscape gliding by outside the car window. ARLANDA CITY she read on an enormous sign outside something that looked like a space station.

"That city grew up almost overnight some years ago," Britta explained. "It's there to accommodate travelers. It has hotels, shopping, restaurants—that sort of thing."

They left behind the enormous glass structures and lights, and the landscape outside the car window transformed from urban to rural in a matter of minutes, with horses, cows, and red barns replacing the cityscape near the airport.

Calista listened to Bengt and Britta telling her about the things she would see and do while she stayed with them, but their voices grew fuzzy and her head was sinking toward her chest, her thoughts drifting....

Her head jerked up when the Toyota slowed to a stop. Calista glanced at her watch. It was three thirty. She had slept for almost half an hour. Outside the car, a beige building as long as a city block stretched along the narrow suburban street. All the windows and the front doors of the building had light blue trim, and tall wooden fences separated tiny front yards from one another. Calista turned to look around. They were, she noticed, in a maze of beige

buildings, another one on the other side of the street and yet another farther away in the distance. How would she find her way home when she left the house to go somewhere? she wondered. All the buildings were identical.

"Row houses," Bengt said, noticing her gaze. "We build a lot of row houses in this country. It feels like you have your own home, but it doesn't take up as much space, and you share one or two walls. It's more energy efficient."

A blue-and-yellow Swedish flag fluttered from a pole on the tiny porch of the row house in front of which Britta parked. "We put the flag out for you, Calista," Bengt called as he lifted her luggage from the trunk of the car.

A lit star hung in the downstairs window, and when Calista glanced toward the second floor, she noticed that there were stars in all the upstairs windows as well. In fact, every home in the row had stars in their windows, almost identical to the Öhströms' star.

"Does that symbolize the star of Bethlehem?" Calista asked.

Britta looked surprised. "I suppose it could," she said. "Maybe that's how it started. I always assumed we had them because it's so dark in Sweden this time of year."

Inside, the house was warm and smelled of tulips. Calista found herself in a perfectly planned entryway with a mirror and a coat and hat rack to her left, and a closet to her right. Underneath the coatrack was a space for shoes and boots. An umbrella rack was mounted on the wall as well. Suzanne would be in heaven with this kind of organization, she thought.

From the entryway Calista could see into the living room. A small Christmas tree stood by the back wall, decorated only with tiny red bows, a few strands of silver garland, and those same tiny white lights she had seen on the Christmas tree in the arrival hall at the airport.

"We take our shoes off in the house, Calista," Britta said with a smile. "Most Swedes do."

"Oops! Of course." Calista had made it almost all the way onto the impeccably polished hardwood floor in the living room with her dirty tennis shoes on. She should have remembered. Jonas had told her about not wearing shoes in the house.

"It's okay," Bengt said when he saw Calista's flustered face. "If we visited you in Moon Lake, we'd automatically take our shoes off in your house, and that would probably be as odd as leaving them on here."

Bengt showed Calista upstairs to a tiny green bedroom with a view of the narrow street that wound its way between the row houses. A low bed covered with a quilted bedspread stood in one end of the room. There was a wooden desk with a laptop computer that Bengt invited her to treat as her own, a small bookshelf crammed full of books, and a floor-to-ceiling dresser.

After Calista had deposited her suitcase and backpack on her bed and used the bathroom, she joined Bengt and

Britta for an early supper in the dining room.

Lit candles were arranged on the table, and a red-and-green pot with three blooming tulips and a tiny Santa Claus stood in the middle. Bengt and Britta seemed to have their places, and Calista waited to see which chair would remain empty. There, the one closest to the red reindeer Christmas curtains and the windowsill crowded with red geraniums seemed to be meant for her. She glanced out the window as she sat down. It was only four thirty P.M. but already pitch-black outside.

"How are you holding up?" Bengt asked, passing Calista a ceramic dish of cauliflower-and-ham stew and a bowl of green salad. "You must be exhausted."

"It's not bad," Calista said. "It's so exciting to be here, I don't think I could go to sleep even if I tried. Besides, the longer I stay up, the quicker I get on your schedule."

"That's a good attitude," Britta said. She moved to pass Calista a pot of boiled potatoes, but suddenly paused. "Say, did your S.A.S.S. advisors in America warn you about boiled potatoes?"

"No," Calista said, laughing. "But I love boiled potatoes, and any other kind of potatoes for that matter."

"Good," Bengt said as Britta passed the potatoes to Calista, "because Swedes eat them with lunch and supper almost every day."

"That'll work for me."

As they began eating, a comfortable silence settled over

them. This might be a good time to tell Bengt and Britta about Jonas, Calista thought. But somehow she couldn't get the words out. What was the most normal thing in the world suddenly felt like a big secret.

Instead of talking, Calista focused on eating. Britta's stew was a welcome improvement over the airplane food.

Despite Britta's protests that it was Calista's first day here and she should take it easy, Calista helped clear the table after supper.

"Help," she gasped when she opened the cabinet under the kitchen sink to discard an empty milk carton. An assortment of bins and boxes and bags crowded the small space. "Which one is the trash?"

Britta laughed. "It took us a long time to get used to it, too, when they started mandating that we sort our garbage, but you'll learn quickly.

"Leftovers go in this biodegradable compost bag on the inside of the door," she said. "Milk cartons and other paper products go in this bin, aluminum cans in this one, colored glass products in this box, and clear glass in this one. Batteries go here, and newspapers over there."

"To an untrained person, a newspaper might look like a paper product," Calista said, laughing. "I didn't think sorting trash would be my most challenging experience in Sweden. But I'm more convinced by the second that my mom would love this country. Landfills are one of her greatest concerns in life."

"Your mom sounds like an interesting woman, "Bengt said. "I remember that your S.A.S.S. application said she's a potter, too, right?"

"Yeah," Calista said. "And she loves music, all kinds of music."

"What about your dad? What's he like?" Bengt asked, continuing to clear the table.

"He's a potter like my mom, but in his spare time, he likes to watch football, or any kind of sport, actually. He also gets excited when I date athletes because he finally has someone to talk to about sports."

"Wow," Britta said. "That would be enough to make me want to date a nerd—like Bengt," she added with a wink.

"Hey, I ski and skate," Bengt said. "And look at these." He flexed his pale, sinewy arms. Britta and Calista laughed.

"I think Dad had hoped for athletic kids, but instead he got Suzanne and me," Calista said. "Neither of us is interested in playing sports, though I kind of like watching some of them. Anyway, Dad gets the second best, my boyfriends, since my twin sister Suzanne doesn't date very much. She just plays the piano."

"Hm, guess you'll have to find yourself a Swedish athlete," Britta said, winking, "to please Dad."

That was the perfect opportunity. Now she'd tell them. Calista opened her mouth, but Britta was quicker.

"Oh, I'm sorry, Calista," she said. "We're so excited to have you here that we're forgetting to be polite. You must be exhausted. Feel free to take some time to unpack and shower if you want to. We can talk more tomorrow."

Grateful, Calista headed upstairs to find some clean clothes and head for the shower.

"Tomorrow, when you're rested, we'll take you to Skansen," Britta called after her. Calista smiled. She couldn't have hoped for a more enthusiastic and welcoming host family. Jonas would love them. But what the heck was Skansen?

Chapter Three

Amazingly, Calista felt totally rested when she opened her eyes the following morning. Not being woken up by Suzanne's before-school piano practice had already helped her state of mind. She shot out of bed and went downstairs to join Bengt and Britta for breakfast in the dining room.

"Are we going to that Skansen place today?" she asked as soon as she saw them. "And what exactly is it?" She unfolded the map of Stockholm that she had printed off the Internet before leaving home. "And *where* is it? Is it close to the castle? My mom said all the public museums in Sweden are free, so could we stop at the National Museum, too? Is it nearby? I read on the Internet that they have an exhibit about Astrid Lindgren, the woman who wrote *Pippi Longstocking.*"

When Calista stopped talking, she noticed that Bengt and Britta were smiling broadly. "Wow, you seem rested," Bengt said.

"And ready to go," Britta added. "We started eating because we figured you'd be sleeping in."

"Yes," Bengt said. "We can stop by both the National Museum and the Royal Palace. We'll be driving right by them. And Skansen is an open-air museum with hundreds of traditional Swedish buildings, a zoo, and, in the summer, gardens. You have to see it."

"Open air, as in *outside*," Calista wondered aloud. "Isn't it cold today?"

"It isn't too bad. It is about minus five degrees Celsius," Bengt said. "In Fahrenheit that's…Britta, help out here, please."

Britta's face lit up. "Hm…twenty-three degrees Fahrenheit."

Calista cheered. "You're an amazingly fast thinker."

"It's just a matter of practice," Britta said modestly.

Calista sat down. She felt ravenous. A cup of steaming tea was poured for her, and Bengt and Britta had made liverwurst sandwiches with sliced cucumbers.

"Help yourself," Britta said.

Calista took a sip of the hot tea and bit into the sandwich. *"Kan vi prata svenska idag?"* she said. Can we speak Swedish today?

"Bra idé," Britta said. Good idea.

While Britta finished reading the paper and Bengt took a shower, Calista went up to her room and logged onto the Internet to check her messages and send a note to Jonas letting him know she had arrived. She hadn't gotten a message from him yet, but she was happy to see that Leah had e-mailed her.

Från: leahwinter@email.com

Till: Calista@email.com

Ämne: Waiting for mail

Cal,

Time to write your friends, girl! That card we gave you was so you'd remember us. Do you have it on your desk? (Do you even have a desk? Maybe you live in an igloo. LOL)

Since you seem to have temporarily misplaced your memory card, here comes a reminder—Leah Winter, 16, from Moon Lake, Wisconsin, shockingly beautiful, stunningly intelligent, amazingly kind to orphans and the elderly, is one of your two best friends in the world, and is waiting for a sign of life from you!

I'll let Sammie remind you of Sammie. I'm sure I wouldn't

do her justice. Btw, Sammie sends her love and says to tell
you Jonas isn't everything.

Anyway, are you speaking Swedish with your host family? What are they like? When do you start school?

Hope you're having fun. Miss ya.

XOXO,

Leah

Calista sighed. What was *that* about? That was exactly the
kind of comment she would have expected from Suzanne,
not from her friends.

Calista hit the reply button.

Från: Calista@email.com

Till: leahwinter@email.com

Ämne: Waiting for mail

Leah,

Miss you, too, though I've only been gone for one day! I
DO remember you. Not to worry.

What's up with Sammie telling me Jonas isn't everything? I *know* Jonas isn't everything. You guys don't need
to worry about it. Sammie just hasn't forgiven Jonas for
standing me up that *one* time. It wasn't on purpose. He
just forgot.

Bengt and Britta are nice. You'd like them. In a few
minutes, they're taking me to this open-air museum called

Skansen. I haven't been speaking much Swedish yet, but we're starting today. Jonas is taking me out for New Year's. I'll try to speak only Swedish with him.

Lv and ksss,

Calista

PS Tell Sammie her comment about Jonas *really* annoyed me. Which reminds me—Sammie was the one who first introduced Jonas to me and said we'd make a great couple, *even though I was going out with Jeff at the time.* I only agreed to go on a date with Jonas because Sammie suggested it. And now she's complaining....

"*Vill du åka nu?*" Britta asked when Calista came downstairs.

"Hm," Calista said, holding her index finger up. "*Vänta.*" Wait, wait, wait, she thought. She flipped through her dictionary. Do you want to go now? she translated. "*Ja,*" she said, grinning.

In the car on their way downtown, Bengt told Calista, in his funny Swedish-English mix, about everything they saw outside the window. He pointed out the enormous high-rises that housed Vattenfall, the state-owned energy company where Britta worked, the train following the side of the highway, and the bridge crossing Lake Mälaren, which brought them into the city of Stockholm.

Calista stared in awe. Mostly, she was impressed with

how orderly and clean everything looked. There was no trash on the side of the road, and everything looked very organized. All the houses in each neighborhood were exactly the same size and were spaced evenly with the same size yards. And, as Bengt and Britta pointed out, row houses were the housing of choice.

Why had Calista thought Stockholm was a quaint little town? It was enormous, and just as metropolitan as Minneapolis and Milwaukee, with too much traffic and too many people.

When they reached the east side of the city, there were fewer buildings, though the ones that were there were enormous. On the north side, from where they came, Calista had noticed many public parks and open spaces, but out here trees grew everywhere, and open fields stretched as far as you could see.

"Ambassadors' homes," Bengt said, nodding toward the mansion-sized houses on the side of the road. Then he burst out "Yes" so suddenly that Britta and Calista both jumped. "A parking spot. It's hard to find parking here, and Skansen is just across the road," he explained. He carefully parallel-parked the car.

The three of them got out and crossed the street, making their way to a ticket booth next to a spiky black iron fence.

Inside the fence, Calista found herself in a strange kind of park, mountainous and wild. Yet, even with the thin

snow cover, she could tell it was landscaped with streams, rocks, and gardens.

The path they were following led to an odd-looking building. Inside, a steep escalator reached up for what seemed like miles, spanning the entire side of a mountain. The walls on the sides were covered with signs advertising an aquarium, a terrarium, and other Skansen attractions.

When they got off at the top of the escalator and walked outside, it felt like they had been transported back a hundred years in time. Along several walking paths were full-sized replicas of traditional nineteenth-century Swedish homes. The old-fashioned tiny red buildings had flat red tile or grass roofs. On one of the roofs Calista could see two tiny, sure-footed goats digging holes in the snow to get to the dead grass underneath.

Hand-lettered signs pointed the way to different animal exhibits—seals, moose, brown bear, lynx.

"Almost all of the animals here are native to Scandinavia," Britta told her. "Let's see some of them after we explore the cabins."

"Oh, we can go inside of them?" Calista asked, excited. How come Jonas had never told her about Skansen? This was exactly the kind of Swedish culture and history that she had always asked him to tell her more about. It would have been a cool place to come with him.

The first building they entered was one of the larger cabins. A fire was roaring in an iron stove, and a man wearing an apron took something out of the fire with a pair of black tongs. The walls in the cabin were covered with heavy, ancient-looking iron tools. A group of tourists was standing behind a rope, watching.

The man took a lump of something blazing hot and put it at the end of a long, thin tube. He blew into the tube and, with a tool he held in his right hand, created a beautiful glass vase. Amazing. Calista had never seen a glassblower at work, but it wasn't unlike what her parents and Suzanne did with clay. They could take an insignificant lump of gray mud and make something beautiful out of it.

Calista was so fascinated with the glassblower that it was hard for Britta and Bengt to get her to go to the next cabin.

"You'll enjoy the next place, too," Bengt promised.

The three of them visited an old-fashioned bakery, a candle maker, a man etching postage stamps, a spinner, a weaver, and a candy maker.

When they had seen a good number of the cabins, they went to look at some of the animals that were outdoors despite the cold: seals, penguins (so not native to Scandinavia, Calista thought), moose, and arctic foxes. Then Bengt and Britta took Calista for lunch at Solliden's Restaurant, which had an incredible view over the waterfront of Stockholm.

"This is a cool place," Calista said, taking a bite of her *Janssons frestelse*, a potato dish with anchovies and

cream. "Thank you for bringing me here. No wait, I can say it in Swedish." She flipped the pages in her dictionary. *"Tack för att ni tog med mig hit."*

Bengt and Britta smiled at her. This would be a good time to tell them about Jonas, Calista thought, wondering why it was so hard.

"Um," she began. Why did she feel so guilty? This was ridiculous. It's not like she'd done anything wrong. "I have this boyfriend, Jonas," she said. "He lives in Stockholm."

Bengt and Britta's eyebrows shot up to their hairline. "How fun!" Britta said. "Where did you meet him? And when do we get to see him?"

"Soon, I hope," Calista said, relieved at the positive reaction. "He was an exchange student at my school in Moon Lake. That's where we met."

"Anytime you want to have him over, Cal, is fine with us," Bengt said, smiling. "Is he athletic? Dad approved?"

Calista laughed. "Definitely, yes. He's a champion soccer player, and he and Dad are really close. And he got along well with my mom." No need to go into detail about how Jonas and Suzanne didn't really hit it off.

"It's great when it works out like that," Britta said.

Calista nodded. She'd been lucky to find Jonas. And even luckier that he had encouraged her to have this already amazing experience in Sweden.

• • •

On the way back from Skansen, Bengt stopped at the National Museum.

"This is enormous," Calista said, walking up the large staircase in front of the building. "I thought we could just zip in and out."

"We can," Britta said. "We can see the Astrid Lindgren exhibit and come back some other time if you want to see more but are too tired today."

Inside, the enormous hall was littered with white, armless statues. The checkered marble floor made Calista feel like donning a ball gown and twirling.

"The National Museum is the largest art museum in Sweden," Bengt said, "built in Florentine and Venetian Renaissance style. But I guess you could see that."

Calista smiled gratefully. "I wouldn't have known the style," she said. "My art history's a bit rusty."

"It holds more than sixteen thousand permanent pieces," Bengt continued. "The museum's also in charge of the art collections of some of the castles, like Drottningholm's Castle, where the royal family lives."

Bengt made a great tour guide, Calista thought. He obviously knew a lot about Stockholm. "The building looks antique," she said.

"It was built in the mid-1860s. In fact, most of the buildings on this peninsula, called Blasieholmen, were built around that time. When the museum opened in 1866, it

was one of the first public art museums in the world."

They found the Astrid Lindgren exhibit on the second floor. Calista enjoyed seeing the writer's original manuscripts, the Danish illustrator Ingrid Vang Nyman's funny illustrations of Pippi Longstocking, as well as Ilon Wikland's astute artwork in most of Lindgren's other books.

"I had no idea she had written this many books," Calista said. "I only knew of *Pippi Longstocking* and *The Brothers Lionheart.*"

"Lindgren is one of the most popular children's writers in the world," Bengt said. "In fact, children's literature is a considerable part of Swedish export to other countries, thanks to her. And she was an amazing woman who donated enormous amounts of money to children's causes."

As they walked out on the steps of the National Museum, Calista couldn't help drawing in a huge happy breath. The city of Stockholm with its glittering waterways lay at her feet. Across the water she noticed an enormous square building with two large wings, its entrance guarded by two golden lions shining in the late-afternoon sun.

"What's that building?" Calista asked.

"That," Bengt said, "is the Royal Palace. This is the perfect place to see it. Actually, there used to be another castle where this one is. It was called Tre Kronor, or Three Crowns. It burned down. Some people think the fire started in an illegal bar in the attic."

"Even from this far away, the castle looks enormous," Calista said.

"It has more than six hundred rooms," Britta noted. "I think it's the largest castle in Europe still in use."

"I thought the royal family didn't live there."

"No, they live in Drottningholm. But this castle houses their offices. This is where they receive dignitaries and conduct their business."

Calista nodded. She was starting to feel a little tired from all the sightseeing. She wanted to get back to the row house to connect with Jonas…and to get some sleep.

It took longer driving home from the city than it had getting there. "Rush-hour traffic," Bengt sighed. Calista felt her head growing heavier.

"Let's see," Bengt said. "It's seventeen o'clock here. That makes it ten in the morning in Wisconsin. No reason whatsoever to be tired." He winked at Calista in the rear-view mirror.

Back at the house, Calista immediately checked her e-mail, hoping for a message from Jonas.

Nothing.

What was wrong? She sent Jonas another e-mail, then called his cell phone. When he didn't answer that either, she sent him a text message. Even if he was still on vacation, he would have his cell phone, she reasoned.

Calista walked downstairs to join Britta in front of the TV

in the living room. Together they watched *Friends* reruns until Calista couldn't keep her eyes open any longer.

The next day Calista took a walk in the neighborhood with Bengt and Britta, practiced her Swedish, tried at least twenty different kinds of Swedish candy, called her parents, and tried to get in touch with Jonas to no avail.

When Calista came downstairs on the morning of her third full day in Sweden, Bengt poured her a cup of coffee. *"Gott slut,"* he said.

"Gott sle-ute?" she tried to repeat. She sipped the strong black coffee, and started spreading orange marmalade on her toast. He could not have said what she thought he said. She set her toast aside and looked in her dictionary. "Happy ending?"

Britta, stepping out of the downstairs bathroom with a towel around her head, laughed. "Yes. That's what we say here on New Year's Eve," she explained. "Morbid, isn't it?"

Calista laughed. "It sounds like an invitation to go jump off a cliff," she said. Their talk about New Year's reminded Calista of Jonas again. "Any messages for me?" she asked casually.

"No messages," Britta said. "Were you expecting a call from Jonas?"

"Um, yeah, but he's probably out of town," Calista said, taking a bite of her toast so she wouldn't have to talk.

Britta seemed to understand the short answer. "We would love to have you here for our New Year's Eve party tonight. Our friends are excited to meet you."

"I'd love to meet your friends," Calista said, swallowing her disappointment. Despite the uncomfortable feeling in the pit of her stomach, she found that it was true, she did look forward to the party. Not that she wouldn't have preferred Kaknästornet with Jonas, and maybe he'd still call, but a party at the house sounded fun, too.

To get her mind off of Jonas, Calista threw herself into the New Year's party preparations. All day she worked alongside Bengt and Britta. They made morel-and-cheese-filled tartlets, cheddar crackers, and blueberry pie with vanilla sauce. They cleaned the already immaculate house, shaking the Persian rugs, washing the glass doors between the kitchen and the living room, polishing the wooden table, and dusting the red leather couches. They moved furniture, opened card tables, wiped folding chairs, and shined silver.

At eight thirty, the first guests made their way between the lit torches and down the small front yard to ring the doorbell.

Bengt opened the door and hugged a thin woman in a glittery black dress. "Calista, this is Pär and Frida."

"*Gott slut*, Calista," Frida said, and hugged her as though they were old friends.

"And this is Hanna," Bengt continued with the next arrival.

For the next hour, Calista shook hands and greeted each guest with a *"Gott slut."* Just as she had decided that this was it, that if they were to fit one more suit-clad or glittery-dressed person into the small house, they would have to use a shoehorn, the doorbell rang again. Since Bengt and Britta were both busy in the kitchen Calista ran to the door.

"Gott slut," Calista said as she opened the door. The girl in front of her looked to be Calista's age and was dressed in black from head to toe. Calista quickly counted five piercings and two tattoos. The girl's hair was jet black, clearly a home dye job, her roots revealing Scandinavian blond hair.

"Jag heter Calista," Calista said, and smiled. "Come on in."

The girl didn't smile back but started moving into the house. "Moa," she mumbled, kicking off her combat boots in the hallway.

"We're your neighbors," the woman behind Moa said. "I'm Karin, Moa's mom." In contrast to Moa, Karin had a warm smile and greeted Calista by shaking her hand with both of hers before walking inside to take her shoes off.

Calista was about to close the door when she noticed someone else in the dark behind Karin. As he stepped toward the doorway, Calista's mouth fell open. The guy who arrived with Moa and Karin was tall and broad-shouldered. His brown hair was a little too long, falling in his eyes and curling around his ears. Even in the semi-darkness, she could tell that his eyes were a deep, warm brown. He reached out to shake Calista's hand. She was relieved, since she seemed to have forgotten how to do anything but stand and stare. She finally remembered to close her mouth.

"*Hej!* My name is Håkan," he said. He smiled broadly at her. "Moa and Karin told me they were getting an American neighbor."

Calista's paralysis finally let go, and she smiled. "I'm Calista," she said, shaking his hand. "Did anyone ever tell you that you look like Prince Carl Philip?" *Oops, I can't believe I just said that,* she thought, using all her willpower not to fling her hands in front of her mouth.

"Is that a good thing?" Håkan asked, smiling. His smile was a little lopsided, as if they had a secret together.

"Ah, yeah, or, I mean," Calista blundered on. She'd be insulting him if she said no, and she would be giving him an embarrassingly huge compliment if she said yes. She shrugged her shoulders. "Oh, I don't know," she said vaguely. "I guess it depends on what you think of Carl Philip."

A cold shiver ran up her back, and she realized Håkan hadn't closed the door behind him. "The door," she said, then, in a kinder tone of voice when he spun around and

pulled it closed, "Can I get you something to drink?"

But Moa had beaten her to it and was already by Håkan's side offering him a cup of cider. "Britta told my mom you have a Swedish boyfriend," she said to Calista, her chin a little lifted, making it more of a question than a statement. "How come you're not with him on New Year's?"

"I, eh…" Calista started. "I haven't gotten hold of him yet." Suddenly she wished Jonas were there so she could show him off.

Moa nodded, then, disinterested, grabbed Håkan's shirtsleeve and pulled him into the almost impenetrable crowd in the living room.

Before Calista had time to duck away, Britta's aunt Pernilla, who was wearing a long red dress, appeared next to her and held out a glass of cider, which Calista accepted. "*Pratar du svenska,* Calista?" Pernilla said loudly, waiting a beat between every word as though Calista was hard of hearing. Then, just to be sure, she translated. "Do you speak Swedish, Calista?"

Calista nodded. *"Lite grann,"* she said, as loudly as Pernilla had addressed her.

"Come over here, Calista!" It was Håkan, clearly trying to rescue Calista from Aunt Pernilla. "Help us pick out some music. I vote for something that the old guys will like, but that won't make us gag." He motioned with his head to Bengt standing next to him.

"I'll teach you 'old guys,'" Bengt said, threatening Håkan with an olive-adorned toothpick.

"Like," Håkan went on, unfazed, "Magnus Uggla or Stina Nordenstam. Moa argues for Sisters of Mercy or The Cure."

"Sorry," Calista said, "I won't be much help. I don't know any of those, but I'm game for anything, preferably something Swedish." She took a sip of her cider, which she realized was spiked.

"Hey, that's one vote for me," Håkan said. "Though I was hoping you'd suggest some American music."

Moa looked bored. It must not have been her idea to involve Calista in the conversation.

"How about we start with something Swedish, an appetizer?" Håkan held up a CD featuring a woman with a crew cut on the cover, then slipped it into the CD player. "Here's Marie Fredriksson," he said, pretending to hold a microphone in front of his mouth. "Don't you just love her sleepy 'after the storm' voice? It's nine thirty P.M. in our Spånga studio on New Year's Eve. Now to Marie. Enjoy."

Calista laughed. He sounded like a real DJ. It could have been phony or cheesy, but Håkan was actually very good.

"Do you DJ for real?" she asked.

Moa patted her black-lipsticked lips in a pretend yawn and stood to leave. Håkan seemed oblivious to the hint.

"I sub at Radio Stockholm sometimes," he said. "But I'd like to work there full-time."

"Your English is really good," Calista said, having abandoned her resolve to speak only Swedish.

"Thanks. I'd love to DJ in English someday. There are so many cool ways to say things in English."

Calista laughed. "That's how I feel about Swedish...and Spanish...and French. Each language comes with a different mind-set, as though people develop a language that fits their temperament and, in order to learn the language, you have to adopt the culture as well."

Håkan's eyes lit up. "Exactly," he said. "Moa thinks I'm an American wannabe, but it's not about that. It's about understanding another culture in a way you can only do if you go there. Besides, America is the place to be if you want to learn to DJ."

A few times over the next few hours, while talking to Håkan, Calista wondered where Moa had gone. Håkan, on the other hand, didn't seem bothered by her absence. Eventually, Bengt called out from the deck, "Get your coats and shoes and come outside."

"Moa says you're going to Klara Norra Gymnasium with her," Håkan said, standing.

"I didn't know she went there," Calista said. "Do you go there, too? How fun!" She smiled. Then she closed her mouth. What was that about? She was almost jumping up and down with enthusiasm. Luckily, Håkan didn't seem to notice.

"I finished *gymnasium* last spring," he said. "I work in a

computer game store in downtown Gallerian now, waiting to start my military service next fall. You should come see me at the store. It's close to Klara Norra. We could have lunch."

Calista glanced around for Moa but didn't see her anywhere. "You're joining the army?" she asked, steering the conversation away from lunch with Håkan.

"Guys over eighteen have to do military service in Sweden. Actually, I could probably get out of it if I wanted to. People do all the time. I just haven't bothered. My dad wants me to go."

"Then what?"

"Then, after I demob, or get out of the army, if I'm really lucky, I'll get a job as a DJ with Radio Stockholm."

They made their way through the sliding-glass doors. Outside, on the deck, the night was clear and the stars bright. Bengt and Britta were pouring champagne into wide-rimmed glasses. Everybody got a glass, including Calista. The loud popping of champagne corks could be heard from porches around them, and in the park behind the house people were moving around in groups.

"Here's to the new year!" Bengt raised his glass, and everybody got quiet. "To getting to know Calista," he said. Everybody looked at her. She glanced at Håkan, who winked. "To new beginnings," Bengt said. Then everybody started counting backward from ten, *"Tio, nio, åtta, sju, sex, fem, fyra, tre, två, ett! Skål!"*

Something exploded above them, and red stars filled the sky. The fireworks began in earnest. The air vibrated with loud explosions, and all over the sky stars erupted as people set off fireworks from their decks.

"*Skål* and Happy New Year," people called, raising their champagne glasses. They began hugging, kissing, and crying. Swedes seemed pretty sentimental about New Year's.

Calista took a sip of her champagne. Ugh, this stuff was overrated. Not sweet like she had expected, but tart, almost sour. Just then, another big bang went off, and it was as if the entire rotunda had broken and tiny pieces of golden sky were floating down onto the earth. Calista couldn't remember seeing fireworks like this before. It wasn't just one or two or even three people setting them off. They came from everywhere.

Her thoughts drifted to Jonas. What would New Year's have been like with him? she wondered. It would have been beautiful to see the fireworks over Stockholm from the tower and to kiss him at the stroke of midnight. But it was fine, she realized, being here at Bengt and Britta's party. She'd see Jonas soon. Still, she couldn't quite shake the feeling of annoyance with him for not letting her know he would be away.

Britta came to hug Calista, tears streaming down her face though she was smiling, then Bengt, then Pernilla, and a lot of people whose names she couldn't remember.

"Gott nytt år," Calista said, remembering the phrase for Happy New Year. Out of the corner of her eye, Calista could see Håkan moving closer. She looked around for Moa again, but she was nowhere in sight. Did she mind that Calista spent so much time talking to her boyfriend?

"Gott nytt år," Håkan whispered, pulling Calista close. His arms felt strong around her. Briefly, his lips brushed against her cheek. Calista released herself from the embrace. *Quick, talk about something neutral,* she thought, something that would stop her heart from banging away.

"What does 'scowl' mean?" she asked.

"Skaal," Håkan said, correcting her pronunciation. He grinned, as though he knew the reason for her question. "*Skål* is the word for a bowl or a drinking vessel, but we use it as a greeting, like 'cheers,' when we drink. I never thought about it before. It's odd, isn't it? As if the Americans would say, 'bowl' every time they took a drink."

The people on the deck began moving into the house again, heading toward the kitchen. About time, Calista thought, her hands and feet thoroughly chilled.

Inside, Bengt instructed them all to line up in front of the stove.

"This is where you'll find out what your new year will be like," Håkan said, standing behind Calista in line. Being close to Håkan kept reminding her of Jonas. "On New Year's, Swedes melt tin. Then they try to interpret the shapes of the tin as it hardens. The shapes are symbols for

what's going to happen in the coming year. It's like reading tea leaves or tarot cards or something like that."

"What do you wish for the coming year?" she asked him.

"You think I'll tell a complete stranger my innermost secrets?" he said, smiling.

"No, I guess not," she agreed. "But I'll tell you my wish. It's not very secret. I want to learn Swedish so well that I'll be able to talk and understand without any problem."

"Good wish." Håkan nudged her. "It's your turn."

Britta was holding out a bowl for her. "These used to be tin soldiers, but they've been melted and reshaped many times," she said. "Here, take one."

Calista looked inside. The bowl was full of tin that looked like finger-sized pieces of crumpled aluminum foil. She pulled a piece from the bowl.

"Now what?" she asked.

"Here, put your piece of tin in the small pan on the stove," Britta said.

"It's melting," Calista said, shaking the pot back and forth like Britta instructed. They waited until the tin had melted, then Britta pointed to a bowl of water on the counter next to Calista. "Now pour the melted tin from the pan into the cold water."

Calista slowly poured the tin into the bowl. "Quicker," Britta said, "or you'll just get a bunch of little pieces. You want to try to get one solid piece."

But it was too late. Calista's tin had congealed into tiny fragments.

"Hm," Britta said, examining the shapes after straining off the water. "Looks like...oh, never mind." She said it too quickly. "Why don't you try again? Pour it quicker next time."

But Calista had already seen it. From the fragments, she picked up the two largest pieces of tin. "Look," she said cheerfully, "if you hold them together, the heart's not broken."

"That's the right attitude." Britta patted her on her back. "And really, you do know that this is just an old superstition anyway."

But there was something unsettling about the broken heart. Even as they were joking and laughing about it, it hung in the air. Håkan was looking at Calista sympathetically. Suddenly, she couldn't stand it. She quietly escaped into the living room, hoping no one noticed her departure, and pretended to look through Bengt's CDs. Why *hadn't* Jonas called her? This wasn't the first time he'd stood her up or forgotten about her, but it was the first time he'd done it after she'd traveled across the world to see him.

When all the guests had had a turn with the tin, they started trickling off. "Hey, where did Moa go?" Bengt asked Karin as she was leaving.

"You know Moa," Karin said. "She hates big gatherings. She left early."

That's strange, Calista thought. Moa hadn't even stayed for the countdown to midnight to be with Håkan.

"I hear you and Moa are both going to Klara Norra," Karin said. "Moa works at a coffee shop downtown for a couple of hours in the morning before school, so, unfortunately, she can't commute with you."

Good, Calista thought, but she smiled at Karin. It wasn't her fault that her daughter was surly and unfriendly.

After everyone left, Bengt, Britta, and Calista cleaned up the house. By the time they finished, it was two A.M.

"I think that was the nicest party I've ever been to," Calista told Britta as she said good night.

When she got to her bedroom, instead of going to bed, Calista logged on to the Internet to send a few New Year's e-mails.

Från: Calista@email.com
Till: Lenawarren@email.com
Ämne: Gott Nytt År

Hej Lena och Gott Nytt År!
Jag är trött nu... oh, forget it. I'm exhausted, is what I wanted to say. I'm not even gonna try to write in Swedish. It's after two in the morning and the first day of the new year. Bengt and Britta had a big party. I spent most of my

time with this guy, Håkan, my neighbor Moa's boyfriend. Nice guy (as in *very* nice and *very* cute).

Through some stupid misunderstanding, I haven't talked to Jonas yet. I think he may be at his cabin. I'm so ready for him to come back so I can chew him out for not being around for New Year's.

School starts on Tuesday. I'm scared silly—wish you were here so I could dig my nails into your hand—it's tradition with us. I'll call you Tuesday night.

ttyl,

Calista

Från: Calista@email.com
Till: Sammiesam@email.com, leahwinter@email.com
Ämne: Gott Nytt År

Happy New Year, girls! My host family just had the greatest New Year's party with tons of people and really good food and cider. And fireworks in this country are something else, really incredible.

It didn't even bother me that there were only two other people our age at the party. One was my neighbor, Moa, who'll be at Klara Norra (my school) with me. It's pretty obvious that she will not become my new best friend. (She's goth and sort of standoffish.) Her boyfriend, though,

is really cool and kind of hot.

Here's the weird news. I still haven't heard from Jonas. Very strange, but when school starts in two days, he's bound to be back in town again.

Wish you were here to do Stockholm with me. Miss you both. Your card is on my desk.

Luv ya,

Cal

Calista had also received a short Happy New Year e-mail from Suzanne. She should e-mail her, too, she thought. Other than calling her parents to let them know she'd arrived, she hadn't really contacted them. But thinking about what Suzanne would say when she found out that Jonas hadn't shown up for New Year's made Calista cringe. Maybe she'd e-mail her after she got in touch with him. Besides, the party had been fun, and right now she was too tired to deal with Suzanne. Instead, she shut down the computer and climbed into bed. As she drifted off to sleep, she realized that the new year brought the real start of her Swedish adventure—she'd be attending a new school, learning a new language, and making new friends. This was definitely going to be a semester of Swede dreams coming true.

Chapter Four

Calista swatted angrily at the beeping alarm clock until it finally stopped. She stretched and opened her eyes. Tuesday, she remembered, her first day of school. She let herself sink back against the pillows. Jet lag and the New Year's party had been an almost lethal combination. Luckily, she'd had yesterday to recuperate from sleep deprivation, staying in bed late, then helping Bengt and Britta get the house back in order after the party.

She still hadn't heard from Jonas, and the memory of the broken tin heart filled her again this morning. Was she in denial? Was it over? She swallowed. She swung her

legs over the edge of the bed and lifted the blinds with one finger. Even though it was six thirty A.M., it was still pitch-black outside. What little snow they had gotten on the day she arrived was gone. Calista sleepily flipped on the light and booted up the laptop. Maybe something had happened to Jonas and he couldn't get back to her. Maybe he was sick.

She logged in to her e-mail account. She had two messages. A flicker of hope made her wake up a little more. But one was from Lena, saying let's get together soon, and the other from Sammie.

Calista typed in Jonas's address.

Från: Calista@email.com
Till: JonasVonC@email.com
Ämne: Where are you???

Jonas,
Var är du??? Could you please get back to me? I'm getting worried about you. Are you okay?
Cal

Then she read her message from Sammie.

Från: Sammiesam@email.com
Till: Calista@email.com
Ämne: Gott Nytt År

Happy New Year to you, too! I'm glad you're having a great time—though don't have too great a time without us, okay? I'm also glad your goth girl neighbor's not your new best friend, since Leah and I kind of like the job.

I'm relieved you're not mad at me for the Jonas comment, and I'm sorry you haven't talked to him yet. You will, I'm sure. I know it's none of my business, Cal, but I wasn't talking about the time he stood you up. I was mad about the time he got drunk after scoring ten goals against Amery and kissed Rosemary Carlson....

Nothing new here. School's started again, and I've been working in your parents' shop, helping Suzanne glaze pottery. Thanks again for setting me up with that job.

I'm totally living through you this semester since nothing, nothing, nothing happens here.

Miss ya,

Sammie

Calista read the message one more time. She did *not* need to be reminded of the Rosemary incident. But there was another thing that bothered her. She had gotten Sammie the job in the shop, but now she wasn't sure she liked the idea of it. It was weird thinking of Sammie spending all that time with Suzanne and not her. Sammie had been one of her best friends since elementary school.

Calista sighed and went downstairs. Bengt was reading the newspaper at the dining room table.

"Good morning, Calista. Please join us at the table," Bengt said.

Calista settled into the same chair she had sat in the evening before.

"Do you want some of the *Dagens Nyheter*?" Bengt motioned to a section of the Stockholm morning paper he wasn't reading. "Coffee?"

"Thanks," Calista said. "Both, please, eh, *ja tack*, I mean." She took the newspaper and surveyed the food set out on the table.

"*Filmjölk,*" Bengt said, noticing Calista's eyes resting on the funny rectangular packages on the table. "I don't know if there's a word for that in English. It's something between yogurt and buttermilk and an excellent way to start the day."

"You sound like an ad," Britta said with a laugh from the kitchen.

"On regular weekdays we usually eat cereal and *filmjölk,*" Bengt continued, "but feel free to help yourself to toast and tea if you don't like it."

Calista poured herself a bowl of *filmjölk*. Then she put cornflakes on top and added a few raisins like Bengt had. She took a bite. It was thick like yogurt, though more tart. Not bad. She helped herself to a piece of hard cracker bread with sweet caviar from a tube, and took the cup of hot coffee Britta handed her. Mm, good. Funny how eating could make you feel so hopeful again. She'd hear from

Jonas today. She knew it. He'd been gone, and now he would be back because school was starting.

Calista flipped through *Dagens Nyheter* to see if she could recognize any of the words. She couldn't. This did not bode well for school.

At seven thirty, she walked out the door, a map of Stockholm in one hand and Bengt's instructions on how to get to Klara Norra Gymnasium in the other.

Though there was no snow on the ground, the sidewalk to the bus was wet and slippery, and Calista had to walk carefully. She made it just in time, reaching the bus stop only a moment before the red bus swung around the corner toward her.

She smiled at the cute bus driver, who didn't look a day over twenty, as she showed him her student pass. He didn't look at her, though, or her pass, and he didn't leave her enough time to sit down before he drove on with a jerk that almost sent her flying down the aisle. She quickly found a seat beside an old woman.

"Hi," she said, smiling. "Is this seat free?"

The woman didn't answer. She pulled her purse onto her lap and stared intently out the window.

Whatever. Calista looked at her directions. Spånga Station. Only five or six stops, Bengt said. She stared out the bus window. Row houses lined the streets, intermingled with parking garages and children's playgrounds.

Soon, the bus swung in front of a large building that

looked like an enormous Wisconsin pole barn. "Spånga Station," the computerized recording said from a loudspeaker. Calista got off, as did most of the others, and was caught in the human flood pouring up the stairs and escalators and into the blue commuter train building.

Calista watched people show their train passes to a turban-clad man in a booth, before continuing out a small gate to the train platform. She showed her pass, careful not to smile this time.

"Hey, why so serious?" the man in the booth said, and winked. Calista laughed. It was hard to figure out this culture.

It was crowded on the train, but Calista managed to find a seat. Everywhere around her, people were talking on cell phones, *loudly*, as though they were in their own living room. But if she caught someone's eye, they immediately looked away. She settled for looking out the window. As the train traveled through first Spånga, and later Sundbyberg, Calista noticed that the area outside the windows looked older than where Bengt and Britta lived. There were freestanding houses here, not row houses, and they were different from one another—different colors, different sizes, different styles. They passed a horse-racing track, where she saw someone exercising his horse, then factories and warehouses.

The closer to Stockholm Central the train got, the closer together the buildings seemed to be. Now Calista could see water and beautiful tall pastel-colored apartment buildings lining the docks. The train went in and out of tunnels, and outside the city grew busy. "Stockholm Central," announced the computerized loudspeaker.

Calista followed the crowd down the stairs, into the underground, groping for Bengt's map in her pocket as she walked. Bengt had highlighted the way she should walk to get to Klara Norra and told her which exit she needed to take at the Central Station. She tried the other pocket. Not there either. She put her backpack on the ground, bending over it, and got bumped by the never-ending stream of people.

Oh no, she thought. Where is the map? She moved to the side and stuck her hands all the way to the bottom of her pack. Crap, crap, crap! She didn't even know which exit to use, and there were so many. Annoyed, she closed her backpack and straightened up.

"Excuse me!" Calista tried to hail an older woman, who promptly started walking faster without even looking at her. "*Ursäkta.* Excuse me," she addressed a mother, who was holding on to a little boy with one finger buried up to the knuckle in his nose. "Klara Norra Gymnasium?" The mother shook her head and smiled. The boy stared at her, and slowly pulled his finger out. *"Jag heter Joakim,"* he said.

Calista smiled. "Nice name."

She glanced at her watch. Ten minutes before school

started. The walk alone would take ten minutes if she knew the way, which she didn't.

As she finally emerged from the station, Calista almost took a step backward. The city was buzzing around her. Everywhere she looked there were people and cars and buses and bicycles and buildings. An enormous beige building with a SHERATON HOTEL sign on it sat on the other side of the busy street, and taxicabs were double-parked in front of the station doors. *Now there's an idea,* she thought.

Calista checked her coat pockets and breathed a sigh of relief when she found a one-hundred-kronor bill she had exchanged dollars for at the Minneapolis airport. She walked up to the closest cabdriver.

"Will this take me to Klara Norra?" she asked, show-ing him her one-hundred-kronor bill. The man smiled and nodded.

"For you," he said in broken English, "is enough."

It took no more than three minutes to get to Klara Norra, but when the cabdriver dropped her off in front of the tall iron gates, he insisted on the entire one hundred kronor. Calista calculated in her head. What was that, like twelve or thirteen dollars? She opened her mouth to object, but only a puff of cold air came out. She had no idea how much a cab cost in Stockholm. She sighed and paid, but didn't smile back at the driver. Instead, feeling stupid and taken advantage of, she turned and started toward the enormous wooden doors of the castlelike building she hoped was Klara Norra, slipping slightly on the icy cobblestones.

The high school was like no other school Calista had ever seen. The building, Bengt had told her, was more than 125 years old. As Calista neared it, she noticed a group of leather jacket–clad girls smoking next to the entrance. One of them looked familiar. Moa. Calista hadn't seen her since New Year's and still felt guilty about monopolizing her boyfriend, Håkan.

As Calista came closer, Moa's group stopped talking.

"Hi," Calista said, smiling, trying hard to pretend she hadn't just stumbled on the step up to the building. Moa lifted her chin in a greeting, but nobody said anything. They just watched her. Calista said a silent prayer that they hadn't noticed her arrival by taxi, or, even worse, seen her pay one hundred kronor for the ride. She pulled the heavy door open and walked in.

If the building was impressive from the outside, it was even more so on the inside. Calista found herself in a large open hall. The floor was made of speckled marble, and so were the staircases, winding their way up on both sides of her. She looked at the schedule that the Stockholm S.A.S.S. coordinator had mailed to her at the Öhströms' house. There, in the corner of the schedule, she found the classroom number, 108, for her first class of the day, philosophy. It must be on this floor then. Walking to her left,

past the stairs, Calista found herself in an even larger hall than the entry, surrounded by marble pillars.

From here, Calista could see all the way to the ceiling of the building, four floors up. But even more awe-inspiring were the floor-to-ceiling oil paintings. Bengt had told her people came from all over the world to see the Klara Norra murals, which was probably a slight exaggeration, something for which Bengt seemed to have an inclination. She had to admit that they looked cool though. They made her feel like she was going to high school in an art museum.

The classroom doors were squeezed in between the murals. Calista started looking for 108. There was 15 and 22. The hundreds must be upstairs. Odd. She hurried up the stairs and found 108. The door was still open. At least the one hundred kronor had bought her something—being on time her first day of school. She hurried inside and, with a quick glance at the twenty-odd students in the classroom, slid into the chair closest to the door.

Calista's butt had no sooner made contact with her chair than someone came up behind her, touching her shoulder. "Calista! I can't believe it."

Calista turned around and jumped up. "Lena," she burst out as she hugged her. "Why didn't you tell me you were going to Klara Norra?"

"Why didn't *you* tell *me*? There are like a hundred gymnasiums in this town. What are the chances we would be going to the same one?"

"Ehem."

The girls turned to the blackboard, and though Calista didn't catch her words, she had a pretty good idea what the tiny, white-haired woman in the front of the room might be trying to convey. Calista sat down in her desk again, but she couldn't stop smiling, and when she glanced at Lena sitting behind her, Lena was smiling, too.

Though it was difficult for Calista to think of anything other than the fact that Lena was here in Klara Norra, she tried hard to pay attention to the teacher. The tiny woman, who looked like she had come with the building 125 years ago, was chatting away a mile a minute while writing something on the blackboard. *"Teoretisk filosofi,"* it said. That must mean theoretical philosophy, Calista concluded. Then it said *"Praktisk filosofi,"* surely meaning practical philosophy. So far so good. Calista could even understand the next three points on the board, "human beings and their symbols," "community and history," and last, "nature and technology." Many of the words, like those for nature, history, and technology, were similar to words in English. Jonas had told her Swedish and English were both Germanic languages, and that's why they were similar. Still, Calista thought, they were *not* similar enough, and a feeling not unlike panic started fluttering in her stomach when she couldn't catch even half of what the teacher was saying. She had been so sure she could learn Swedish quickly that she had signed up to take almost

all her classes in Swedish. Now she wasn't so confident. Knowing Lena's friendly face was behind her made her feel a little better, though.

Next to the list of topics on the board, the teacher had written another word, "Ripan." What did that have to do with philosophy?

The teacher managed, in no time, to get her dark blue dress entirely covered in chalk. She had turned from the board, still talking very quickly. Understanding her was hopeless.

Momentarily abandoning her efforts to follow the teacher, Calista allowed herself to look around the class-room. Through the chalk cloud she could see that several of the students didn't look anything like the Swedes of her imagination. One looked Arabic, another African. Several students spoke with an accent and one, a young woman with a head scarf, who looked to be at least ten years older than the rest of them, seemed to know even less Swedish than Calista. When the teacher asked her a question, the woman gesticulated wildly and said something in a foreign language—even more foreign than Swedish.

At the end of the lesson Calista had learned nothing, at least nothing about philosophy. She'd better pick up Swedish quickly, she thought, if she wanted to pass her classes. At least they were given only pass or fail grades, or pass with distinction, though Britta said not to bother trying to pass her classes with distinction. It was hard enough if you had been speaking Swedish all your life.

"If we hurry, we'll have time to get coffee or tea before the next class," Lena said as they left the classroom. She put her arm through Calista's and pulled her along down the stairs. "How do you like Ripan?"

"Ripan? Doesn't that mean some kind of bird?" Calista flipped the pages in her Swedish-English dictionary. "Ripan...a ptarmigan?"

"That's the teacher. Her name is Inga Ripberg, but she wants us to call her Ripan. She's always been called that because she's so small and birdlike. A lot of teachers here go by their first names or nicknames."

"That'll take some getting used to," Calista said, smiling. "She seems nice. I just have a hard time understanding her."

They reached the bottom of the stairs and took their place at the end of the long line to the coffee counter. "So how is your boyfriend, Jonas? Have you gotten together yet?" Lena asked.

"No," Calista said. "I'll talk to him tonight." She so did not want to go on about Jonas. "I almost didn't make it here this morning," she said, changing the subject. "I lost the map Bengt made for me and had to take a cab, and the driver charged me one hundred kronor to drive from Central Station to Klara Norra. I felt like such an idiot."

"Why? That sounds like a great idea to me," Lena said. "Taking a cab when you didn't know how to get here was

smart. The cabdriver who overcharged you is the idiot, not you."

Calista nodded, thinking about what Lena had said. Lena was right. It made her feel better.

"Hey! Finally someone who speaks a language I understand."

Lena and Calista turned to look at a girl with generous curves and hair like wildfire. She was wearing a long, flowy skirt over tights and cowboy boots. "I'm Monique," the girl said in a strong southern American accent. She smiled. "I'm here with the S.A.S.S. program. I'm from Alabama." Monique's wide smile, showing perfect white teeth, was contagious.

"I'm with the program, too," Calista said, and smiled back. "And this is Lena. From Sweden," she added.

"Nice scarf," Lena said, and reached out to touch the rainbow-colored scarf Monique had tied around the waistband of her skirt. "Raw silk. Cool."

"I bought it at Myrorna," Monique said. She looked at Calista. "It's a used-clothing-store chain in Stockholm. There's one not far from here."

There were only four people ahead of them now.

"Did you notice the hot guy working here," Monique whispered when they were almost at the counter.

Calista peeked around the people in front of them. The guy at the counter had long blond hair pulled back in a ponytail, blue eyes, and fair skin. "Yeah, he's cute," she said. "I don't look much these days, though. I have a boy-friend." Well, maybe, she thought.

"Oh, come on, girl," Monique said, "looking never hurt anybody."

After they had each gotten a cup of hot tea, they waved good-bye to Monique, who went to her next class. It turned out Lena and Calista had several classes together. After philosophy, they had math, world literature, and French, the latter something Calista had been strongly discouraged from taking since, according to the S.A.S.S. advisor, learning another language in another language could be exceedingly difficult. But Calista couldn't resist picking up another semester of French. She had finished the highest level available at Moon Lake High. She would lose what she had already learned if she didn't continue, she reasoned.

After French class and a lunch of lentil stew and hard cracker bread at the school cafeteria, Lena went off to political science, chemistry, and textile arts, while Calista had Swedish language, followed by Swedish culture—both with Monique—and, lastly, something called body balance.

Of all of her classes, the Swedish culture class was proving to be the most interesting. It had only six students in it, the same six as in the Swedish-language class. The teacher, Kathy, was an American who had lived in Sweden for fifteen years. Other than Monique and Calista, there

were two other exchange students from the United States in the class, and two recent immigrants, the woman with the head scarf from Calista's philosophy class being one of them.

"In this class, I would like *you* to decide what you want to focus on," Kathy said when they were settled in their chairs. "I want you to choose a time period in Sweden that you are interested in learning about this semester. At the end of the semester in May, you will do a presentation not only to our small group, but to some of the other classes as well. Do any of you have an idea of what period you'd like to research?"

Hands shot up all over the classroom as the students quickly picked the Renaissance, the Enlightenment, modern times. Monique picked the 1960s and '70s. Calista was still thinking. Jonas had told her a little bit about the Vikings. They used to inscribe memorial stones in runes, the old Viking letters, for their dead, he had told her. These stones, often more than a thousand years old, were still around in a number of places in Sweden, many of them in the Stockholm area. Jonas had promised to take her to a few of them.

"The Viking era," Calista said when Kathy called on her.

Kathy smiled. "I was hoping someone would choose that. It's an interesting part of Swedish history." Calista nodded and knew that she had picked the right era.

"Why did you pick the 1960s and '70s?" Calista asked Monique when they walked out of class together.

"My grandparents were hippies," Monique said. "They talk so much about those days that it makes me curious. It was probably pretty different in Sweden though."

Calista nodded. "It sounds like a cool project, doesn't it?"

"Mm-hmm," Monique agreed. "Definitely better than solving math problems."

"It looks like being a foreign student is going to have its perks."

After Swedish culture, Calista had body balance. The teacher, Peter, a guy who didn't look much older than the students, promised the class that throughout the semester they would learn at least ten different ways to exercise. The first day they did yoga.

When class was over and Calista walked out the heavy door of Klara Norra, she felt as though she had gotten a thorough workout just getting through her first day of school. It was lucky that she had asked Lena for detailed information on how to get to the train from Klara Norra, or she would have been in trouble again. It was already dark outside. The Swedish language buzzed in her head all the way home. She had been so confident, but now she wondered how she would ever learn.

Calista checked the answering machine in the kitchen

as soon as she got home. Jonas had not left a message. She was grateful that Bengt and Britta were still at work. She went to her room and dialed Jonas's number. Her fingers were shaking so much she misdialed twice before she got it right. After two signals, just when she was ready to hang up, a woman picked up and said something in Swedish.

"Hi, I'm Calista," Calista said in English. It was quiet on the other end. "I'm, eh, a friend of Jonas's, from America," she tried.

The voice on the other end sounded hesitant but kind, and the woman's English was good. "Oh, you're a friend of Jonas. How nice. And you're calling from America?"

Calista felt a lump forming in her throat. Did the woman, Jonas's mother surely, not know that Calista existed and that she had come to Sweden to see him?

"I'm in Sweden," Calista said, her voice squeaky. "Is Jonas there?"

"Oh, no, dear, he's out with friends. Can I take your number and ask him to call you back? He should be home in a few hours."

Calista's head was spinning. Jonas wasn't sick...or comatose. He was out with friends. He had *chosen* not to call her.

"He has my number, thanks," Calista managed, her voice hoarse. Then she clicked the off button.

Calista sat with the phone in her hand, staring at the

window in front of her. It was dark, and all she could see was her own reflection. Why would he do that? she thought, the lump in her throat threatening to erupt into tears. He didn't have to ask her to come to Sweden....She realized that she was freezing. But she didn't move.

Did Jonas ask her to come? Had he *ever* really asked her? Maybe it had all been her doing. He *had* said something about visiting, a long time ago, but it was she who had decided to apply to the S.A.S.S. program so they could be together for an entire semester. Her chest ached. She was shaking. Someone opened the door downstairs, and Britta's voice called out.

"Calista, *hej*. How was your first day of school?"

Calista opened her mouth to answer, and that's when it came, quiet little whimpers at first, then loud, racking sobs. She couldn't get a single word out.

Britta bounded up the stairs without even taking off her shoes. "Oh, *lilla gumman*," she said. "Sweetie, what happened?"

"It's Jonas," Calista managed to get out between sobs. "It's over."

Britta said nothing. Gently, she took the phone from Calista's hand and put it on the desk. She sat down next to Calista, putting an arm snugly around her shoulder, and held her while she cried. They sat like that until Bengt got home a half hour later. By then, Calista felt empty. She let herself be led to the dining room for supper. Bengt looked

concerned, but Calista was grateful that he asked nothing. Britta could tell him later, she thought.

After vegetable soup, boiled potatoes, and Britta's homemade bread, Calista went back to her bedroom and logged on to the net. She'd tell him…something. She didn't know what. But she already had a message. From Jonas.

Från: JonasVonC@email.com

Till: Calista@email.com

Ämne: no subject

My mom said you called. I guess I should have told you sooner—this is not a good time for me to have a girlfriend. Sorry, Cal.

Jonas

Calista stared at the computer screen. That insensitive moron! She couldn't believe Jonas could be so mean. She wanted to scream or throw something. Her hands were shaking. What was it Suzanne had said to her before she left? That she was good at a lot of things? Well, she definitely wasn't good at relationships. This wasn't the first time she'd picked poorly when it came to boyfriends. There was Jeff, and Jared, not to mention Adam from eighth grade, who had broken her heart.

Angrily, she wiped the tears from her cheeks and took a deep breath. She felt like such an idiot. Why hadn't she realized what Jonas was like? It should have been clear to her what kind of person he was. Everybody else saw it, why didn't she?

Maybe this is why she had taken so long to tell Bengt and Britta about Jonas, she thought, because she knew somewhere in the back of her mind that he would dump her. She was completely embarrassed and felt so stupid.

She blew her nose. What would she tell everyone? And what about Dad? He would be so disappointed. She started sobbing again.

Från: Calista@email.com

Till: leahwinter@email.com, sammiesam@email.com

Ämne: You were right

Sammie, Leah,

Jonas broke up with me. Would you believe that I came all this way for him? I'm such an idiot.

Cal

Calista got into bed early, and despite having told herself Jonas wasn't worth weeping over, she cried herself to sleep. In the morning, she found an e-mail from Leah.

Från: leahwinter@email.com

Till: Calista@email.com

Ämne: Jonas

Cal,

I'm so sorry about Jonas. Just forget him. You went to Sweden for more than a worthless boyfriend—remember how you really wanted to learn the language.

And, Cal, you're so not an idiot. I think of you every time I have to do something scary. You have a way of just going in there and doing it, like it's nothing. Like going to Sweden. I could never do that.

Know what? Life without a boyfriend might not be so bad. Look at me (LOL).

Love ya,

Leah

Chapter Five

"Torbjörn, can you help me with this?" Sofia, a short girl in the front row, was waving her hand.

Even after two and a half weeks of classes, Calista had a hard time getting used to students calling their teachers by their first names.

Torbjörn, the math teacher, ran his fingers through the strands of hair that covered his bald spot. He sighed and moved to Sofia's desk.

Lena slid her notebook in front of Calista. There was a message scribbled on it. "Supper at my house tonight?"

Calista glanced toward the front of the room. Torbjörn was still helping Sofia.

"Love to," Calista wrote back. "I have to let Bengt and Britta know, though." Calista passed the notebook back.

"Calista, would you care to share your concerns with the rest of the class, please," a suddenly alert Torbjörn said from the front of the classroom.

"Gärna," Calista said, smiling, while frantically trying to figure out how to save herself. "Lena and I were just wondering how different each proof of the Pythagorean theorem has to be to count as a proof in its own right," she tried in Swedish.

"Okay," Torbjörn said, laughing. A few giggles could be heard from around the room. "Not that I believe for a second that that's what the two of you were writing about, but the fact that you're doing so well with your Swedish, when you've been here less than a month, will get you off the hook this time."

Calista smiled, but a shiver ran down her back. It had been more than two weeks since Jonas broke up with her. Surprisingly, she wasn't too brokenhearted anymore. She still wished she had someone with whom to see the romantic sights of Stockholm, but she didn't really miss Jonas. When she thought of him, it was more with a feeling of irritation—he shouldn't have dumped her like that.

Somehow, Calista had managed to avoid telling her family about Jonas. In fact, she hadn't even responded to an e-mail Suzanne had sent to her last week. Suzanne's jabbering about practicing and recitals and helping at the pottery store with Sammie only annoyed her. Calista sighed and shrugged off her feelings of guilt and irritation, something that seemed to pop up every time she thought about Suzanne these days.

In Swedish culture class Monique sat down next to Calista as usual.

"Hey, Monique," Calista said. "How's your project going?"

Monique piled a stack of books about the Vietnam War on her desk. "Pretty good. I had no idea how involved the Swedes were in antiwar protests in the 1960s and '70s."

"Really?" Calista said. "From what I've read about the Viking period, they didn't seem quite so peaceful back then."

"I'm learning a lot," Monique said, "but I still wish there was a little more time for fun and a little less need for studying."

The last of the students had arrived and were finding their seats.

"I've been meaning to ask you something," Monique went on. "My host sister, Marie, and I are having a party this weekend," she said. "Would you like to come? Lena will be there. The other S.A.S.S. students in the area are coming, too, including Cory, the guy I told you about, and a

few friends of Marie. I don't know if you've met Marie yet. She's a senior here at Klara Norra. Anyway, we're having a *julgransplundring*."

"A *julgrans* what?" Calista asked.

Monique laughed. "I'm still trying to understand it myself."

"*Julgransplundring* is when you say good-bye to Christmas," said their teacher Kathy, who had overheard them. "Literally, it means the plundering of the Christmas tree. You basically strip the tree and throw it out in the yard."

"Interesting," Calista said. Then she turned to Monique. "Of course, I would love to come, *julgransplundring* or no *julgransplundring*. I'm always up for a party. But…do you still have your Christmas tree?"

"Yeah, my host mom said she wanted to make sure we Americans get to see a real *julgransplundring*."

Kathy laughed. "Swedes celebrate Christmas forever," she said, "until there is something else to celebrate." She turned to the rest of the class. "Let's get back to work on our projects," she said. "Today will be another of our in-class research days."

Calista pulled out her book about women during the Viking era, and started taking notes.

"Look at this," she whispered to Monique. "This is so unfair. The Viking-era women had strong positions in society when the men were out gallivanting and travel-

.ing the world. The women could own and inherit land, get a divorce, and even fight battles. But only one in ten rune stones was raised for or by a woman. And, listen to this, even though they were instrumental in bringing Christianity to the Nordic countries, when Christianity became the dominant religion, women's roles took a nosedive, and they lost a ton of status."

"That's only because we weren't around to throw a fit," Monique said.

Calista laughed and bent over her books again.

At the end of the day, instead of going to the commuter train, Calista headed for the subway with Lena. She borrowed Lena's cell phone and called Bengt and Britta to let them know she wouldn't be home for supper.

Lena lived in a villa in Hässelby, the last stop on the subway line from the city.

Like much of Stockholm, Hässelby Strand was situated on Lake Mälaren. The lake's long tendrils of water seemed to reach everywhere. Even though Calista lived in Wisconsin, a state littered with freshwater lakes, she found it amazing that the entire city of Stockholm, even the suburbs, was surrounded by water. In Wisconsin, they had Lake Superior and Lake Michigan, but they were on the outskirts, not so intimately interwoven with the cities on their shores.

As they got off the subway in Hässelby, Calista noticed several apartment buildings situated on the summits above

the lake. "Those people must have an incredible view," She said. "In Wisconsin, only rich people would live like that, but those don't look like expensive apartment buildings."

"They're not. Anyone can live there," Lena said.

The girls followed the walking path snaking its way along the wooded areas next to the lake. A cold wind blew off the lake, and Calista zipped up her coat. The ground was powdered with snow again, and ice covered the lake.

"Don't you just love how pretty snow makes everything look?" Lena said. "And how it attaches differently to different things. It's like magic."

"Eh, yeah. I guess I never thought much about it," Calista said. It did look cool now that she paid attention. In the lingering daylight, she bent low to admire tiny piles of snow on each tiny piece of gravel.

Lena's house was a ranch-style white-tile villa. Like almost all the free-standing houses Calista had seen in Stockholm, it was surrounded by a tiny yard and a red picket fence. Swedes seemed to be fond of fences, Calista thought, especially red ones.

She followed Lena up the steps to the front door. A tall, bald, black man met them in the entryway.

"*Hej,* Calista," he said. *"Hur mår du?"*

"Jag mår bra," Calista said.

"Very good. You're already speaking Swedish."

"This is my stepdad, Felix," Lena said. "He has a funny accent because he's from southern Sweden."

Calista smiled. She had just been thinking that Felix was a little difficult to understand.

"Hey," the man said, "you guys from Stockholm are the ones who speak funny. In Skåne we speak *standard* Swedish."

Calista realized she didn't know that much about Sweden yet. It was probably time she did away with her preconceived notions about what Swedes should look like and be like. They weren't all blond and blue-eyed, and they weren't anywhere near as shy as she had thought, unless you met them on the train, in which case you should not smile or talk to anyone, she'd learned. But if you were in someone's home, or in class with them, Swedes were as talkative and friendly as any Americans she knew.

Calista and Lena took off their coats and shoes in the roomy hallway and followed Felix into the living room. Like in Bengt and Britta's home, it was nicely furnished in blond wood, with original art on the walls. The Warréns seemed to favor nature paintings—one painting showed a field of tulips, another an autumn forest scene, and a third a sailboat on a summer lake. They also had an elaborate sound system with hidden speakers, and several floor-to-ceiling bookshelves.

One wall of the Warrén living room was covered with windows framed with white lace curtains. Through the windows Calista could see a bike path winding its way between the houses in the back. Those bike paths were

everywhere, and even now, in January, they were crowded with bikers dressed in reflective clothing and bike helmets.

Lena's mom joined them in the living room, wearing an apron and carrying a tray. She wiped one hand and held it out to Calista. "*Hej,* Calista. *Välkommen.* I've been looking forward to seeing you again."

She offered the girls and Felix tiny sandwiches with cream cheese, cucumber, and a thin slice of lemon.

"Would it be impolite to take, like, ten?" Calista asked Lena after trying one.

"Yes," Lena said, "but my parents wouldn't mind if you were impolite because you love their food. Go ahead."

"Calista, tell me about your family," Felix said, munching on a sandwich.

"Hm." Calista chewed slowly and took a sip from her glass of sparkling water. "My parents are potters," she said. "They own a workshop where people take classes or glaze their own pottery. It has a coffee shop attached to it, and a store where they sell pottery and other artwork."

"Artists, huh," Felix said, "the most interesting sort of people. I'm sure you've seen Lena's work."

"No," Calista said, surprised. She turned to Lena. "How come you didn't tell me you're an artist?"

"I'm not," Lena said. "Felix thinks if you can draw a straight line or paint a dot, you're ready to have your work hang at the National Museum."

Felix laughed. "Show her, Lena," he said. "And let Calista judge for herself."

"Felix," Lena said, exasperated.

"Okay, I'll get it, then," he said.

Felix returned with a roll of fabric that he began to unfurl on the living room couch. Calista gasped. The artwork, a wall hanging measuring about four square feet, was created in layers, using different kinds of fabric and material. The outer layer was mostly made from a sleek, shiny black material, but underneath it, through rips and tears in the black, one could glimpse the richest reds and the most shimmering golds. Black-, red-, and gold-colored yarns were skillfully woven around the edges of the artwork. Calista couldn't tear her eyes away.

"It's incredible, Lena. How come you haven't told me about your art before? And why isn't this piece hanging on the wall?"

"She won't let us," Felix answered.

"I'm just playing around," Lena said, her voice irritated. "I'm sure you have things like that, too, things you like to mess around with. Everybody has hobbies."

Calista shook her head. "No," she said, "I can't even do pottery. My mom used to say I must have gotten switched at birth. My twin sister, Suzanne, started throwing pots at three. Even now, I can't throw the stupid lump in the middle of the wheel." Calista smiled. "Are your sisters and your brother artistic, too?" she asked, changing the subject.

Lena shook her head, but Felix interrupted. "They're all artistic," he said. "I don't know why they have to be so modest about it. The oldest, Sandra, interns for the United Nations in Brussels, doing boring stuff like law, but she's really a painter. She needs to go to art school like her younger sister Linn, who does computer animation. Their brother, Niklas, works as a garden designer at a kibbutz in Israel."

"Felix," Pia said sternly from the doorway, "don't bore Cal with the details of our family. Let's eat."

"I'm not bored. It's fascinating," Calista said, rising to follow them into the dining room. "Swedes are so cosmopolitan. You guys move all over the world as though it's your own backyard."

"We have to," Felix said. "Our backyard is too small and crowded."

Calista laughed as she pulled out the chair next to Lena and sat down. Like Bengt and Britta, the Warréns had set their dining room table with lit candles and cloth napkins.

A beeper sounded from the kitchen, and Pia left and returned with a large baking dish filled with sliced, baked potatoes. It smelled deliciously of garlic. Then she brought a bowl of salad and another baking dish with something that looked like a very lumpy loaf of bread, which Felix cut in thin slices. "Baked fillet of pork stuffed with morel

mushrooms," Pia said. "We picked the mushrooms our-
selves."

As Pia and Felix served the meal, Calista was beginning
to realize that this semester would not only be a sightseeing and language-learning adventure, but it would also
include great gourmet dining.

"So where is your sister Linn?" Calista asked Lena
between bites. "I thought she lived at home."

"She's doing something at the university," Lena said.
"She might as well not live here for all we see her."

Lena's mom smiled. "Lena doesn't suffer too much from
having her sister gone."

Lena grinned.

Calista could understand exactly how she felt. Though,
in her opinion, it was much better to be the one who was
gone.

"I like to be alone," Lena said. "I go to our cabin by
myself sometimes. It's just south of the city." She lit up and
turned to Calista. "You should come. It'll be a good Swedish
experience and great for your Viking project. I can't believe
I haven't thought of that before. There's a really old church
in the village with a rune stone in front of it."

"I'd love to go," Calista said. "It sounds like fun! And it
would be great to see the rune stone. I've checked out a
few of them in the Stockholm area. It would be cool to find
one with a different rune alphabet."

"Are there different rune alphabets?" Felix asked, surprised. "In my days, in school, we learned about the futhark. That's not the only one?"

"From what I've learned, the futhark was used only from 200 to 700 A.D. It was called the futhark because the first letters were *f, u, th, a, r,* and *k,* spelling futhark."

"Really?" Lena said. "I didn't know that."

"But in 800 to 1100, they used another alphabet. Then there was yet another one in 1100 to 1500. The confusing thing, of course, is that they're similar but not exactly the same. Most people just call all of them 'Viking runes.'"

"That's interesting, Calista," Pia said. "I can't believe how much you've learned about this in such a short time. You must really enjoy it."

Calista nodded. "I love it." And she realized that she meant it.

When they had finished their meal, followed by coffee and *bondkakor,* a small, hard sugar cookie with almonds, Calista noticed that it was late, even for a Friday night. She called Britta to let her know she was on her way to the bus, but Britta insisted on picking her up.

How could she have been so lucky, Calista wondered, walking toward the subway station, where Britta would be able to find her easily, to have gotten Bengt and Britta for a host family, and Lena for a friend? She felt so comfortable and happy when she was with them. Every day she got to speak Swedish and learn new things. And all this, she thought, surprising herself, because of Jonas. Yes, what he did was low, and she hadn't entirely forgiven him yet, but if it weren't for him, she wouldn't be here.

The next morning, Calista woke early so she would have time to study before going to the *julgransplundring* party at Monique's host family's house in Sollentuna, a suburb north of Spånga. But before she opened her book, she logged on to her e-mail. Another message from Suzanne. And she hadn't even responded to the earlier ones.

Från: Suzic@email.com
Till: Calista@email.com
Ämne: Jonas

Calista, I can't believe you didn't tell me Jonas broke up with you. Sammie mentioned something about it yesterday, when she was working at the shop with me. I pretended I already knew, since I was totally embarrassed that you told the entire world but not your twin sister. And it happened MORE THAN TWO WEEKS AGO. Are you going to tell me about it?
Suzanne

Calista sighed. Even though she and Suzanne were twins, Sammie and Leah had been her closest friends for years, and they were the ones she turned to for support. Suzanne

was usually busy with piano. What would she write back to Suzanne? She remembered not wanting to tell Suzanne about Jonas flaking on New Year's. That seemed small in comparison. And, assuming Suzanne had told their parents about the breakup, she'd have to explain to Mom and Dad about Jonas and about not telling them. It was just too much to deal with now. She'd e-mail them some other time. She logged off and opened her philosophy textbook instead.

Calista had just finished reading Descartes's *Meditations* when she saw Lena walking into the front yard. Bengt beat Calista to the door.

"So this is the famous artist we've heard so much about," Bengt said, smiling widely as he opened the door to let Lena in.

"Definitely not," Lena said. "You must have been expecting someone else."

Calista, walking up behind Bengt in the hallway, laughed. "Someday you'll see her stuff hanging in a museum, Bengt, trust me."

The girls chatted with Bengt and Britta for a few minutes, then left for Spånga, where they would catch the bus to Sollentuna and Monique's party.

Just as they turned off Bengt and Britta's street, a black Saab drove up behind them, honking. Calista peeked in the window and saw Håkan and Moa.

"*Hej,* Calista. Where are you going?" Håkan called out the lowered window.

"Sollentuna," Calista called back, her face heating up.

"Want a ride? I'm taking Moa to Sollentuna Centrum for her band's rehearsal."

Hm. Did she really want to impose on Moa and her boyfriend? But it made no sense for them to wait for the bus when they could have a ride.

Calista looked at Lena, who was mouthing, "Do you know him?" Calista nodded. Lena shrugged her shoulders as though either way was fine with her.

"Sure," Calista said.

The girls jumped in the backseat. "*Hej,* Moa," Calista said. Then, remembering her manners, "Lena, this is Håkan and Moa. Moa is my neighbor." She pondered what she would say about Håkan but couldn't come up with a good way to describe him, so she skipped it. "Håkan and Moa," she said, instead, "this is my friend Lena."

Håkan waved to Lena and smiled in the rearview mirror. Moa responded with a flat hello but didn't turn around to greet them.

"I have a CD I wanted to loan you," Håkan said to Calista, rummaging in his glove compartment with the same hand he used to flawlessly operate the stick shift. Now there was multitasking if she'd ever seen it. He reached back and handed Calista a CD with *Väsen* writ-

ten on the front. "You said you were interested in Swedish music. This is cutting-edge. You should listen to them. They tour the States pretty often."

"What does *Väsen* mean?" Calista asked.

Håkan grinned. "I haven't thought about it before, but the word *väsen* has several meanings. It means 'noise,' but it also means a 'being,' though neither of those English terms even begins to cover the true meaning of the word. I guess it's something of a mix of the English definitions for noise and being—it's a way to describe the true nature of things. Actually, that word is a perfect illustration of what we talked about on New Year's, you know about how language is grounded in thought and culture."

"Words can be so fascinating," Calista said, grinning.

Håkan nodded in agreement. "Do you guys know where we're going?" he asked.

Since Lena was the one with the map, she directed Håkan to Monique's house.

"Thanks for the ride," the girls said as they stepped out of the car. "Nice meeting you two," Lena said. Moa grunted good-bye, and Håkan smiled and waved through his open window before he took off for Sollentuna Centrum.

"You were blushing in the car," Lena said, walking up the path to Monique's house.

"Was not," Calista said, but she was laughing.

"That must be the guy you e-mailed me about, the one

you talked to on New Year's? He seems to like you. Though Moa doesn't seem that friendly."

"Well," Calista said, "Moa's his girlfriend." But she couldn't help throwing a last glance after the black Saab as it pulled around a corner and disappeared.

Monique's house was a small red cottage in a neighborhood of large white villas. The yard surrounding the house was hidden under a thin layer of snow, and the garden was full of knobby apple trees. The windows of the house were lit with the same stars that hung at the Öhströms' house.

When Monique opened the door, Calista smelled cinnamon and apple cider. On a table in the entryway sat a large gingerbread house, expertly built and elaborately decorated with white frosting.

There were maybe ten people in the living room beyond the entryway. Monique's host sister, Marie, a tall girl with her hair cut in a sharp bob, offered Lena and Calista cider and cinnamon rolls when they walked inside. Then Monique went around the room introducing Lena and Calista to the other guests, a few of whom were exchange students, a couple were friends of Marie's who attended Uppsala University, and the rest were Swedish teenagers Monique and Marie knew from the area.

"And this is Cory, a Rotary exchange student from Iowa," Monique said, finishing her introductions and pointing to a

surfer-looking guy who was returning from the kitchen.

"Right. Monique said you'd be here," Calista said, shaking Cory's hand. "We sit together in Swedish culture class."

"Oh, you're the Viking project girl," Cory said.

Calista laughed.

While Lena and Calista found places to sit next to Cory's friend, Mattias, Marie brought in a large tray with the gingerbread house on it and put it on the table in the middle of the room.

"My host mom and dad decided to stay away today," Monique told Calista. "I can't imagine why...." Then she asked, "Calista, do you want to take the first swing?" She handed Calista a hammer that had been sitting on the table.

"A swing? At the gingerbread house?"

Monique nodded.

"That's what we do," Mattias said. He had a pleasant face, short blond hair, a sharp chin, and green eyes. "All gingerbread houses meet the same fate," he said. "Usually they're destroyed sooner, on January 13—twenty days after Christmas."

"Okay," Calista said. "I'll do it." She moved closer to the gingerbread house and lifted the hammer over her head, letting it fall onto the roof. Pieces of gingerbread flew around the room.

"Scary how good that felt," Calista said, laughing.

Mattias laughed beside her, touching her arm playfully. "I wouldn't want to get in the way of that hammer," he said.

Calista felt herself blush.

"Help yourselves," Monique said. She picked up a large piece of gingerbread that had sailed across the room and landed on the windowsill next to her. "You might want to stick with the pieces on the table, though. I don't vouch for the safety of the stuff that's been on the floor."

Monique moved across the room and squeezed down between Calista and Mattias on the couch.

"I guess you've met Calista," she said to Mattias. "She came to see her Swedish boyfriend, and the sorry ass broke up with her when she got here."

Calista's breath caught in her throat, and she raised her eyebrows at Monique.

"Really?" Mattias asked. "That's a bummer."

"Yeah," Monique said, turning to Calista. "He's obviously an idiot since Cal here is the prettiest thing around. Don't you think, Mattias?" she added, winking.

Mattias looked like he was thinking about it, scanning the room. "Yeah, I'd say," he finally agreed.

"Monique!" Calista shrieked. But she couldn't keep from laughing. Monique did have a gift for drama.

"Did you know Mattias is a soccer player?"

Monique turned to Mattias and mock-whispered. "Calista has a thing for soccer players."

Mattias laughed, and Calista rolled her eyes at Monique, who then moved across Mattias to sit on Cory's lap.

"Seriously," Calista asked Mattias. "You play soccer?"

Mattias nodded and was just about to say something when Marie handed them both a sheet of paper that looked like...song lyrics?

Marie started the CD player. *"Nu är glada julen slut..."* they sang along with the stereo. Now happy Christmas is over, Calista translated, picking up the melody and starting to sing along. The Swedes knew the song by heart. While singing, they got up and started stripping the remaining ornaments off the Christmas tree.

"This poor tree should have been out of the house weeks ago," Monique told Calista, who was standing next to her. "My host mom wouldn't hear of us getting rid of it before the party, though."

When the tree was clean of ornaments, they hung sparklers on the bare branches. Calista prayed that the dry tree wouldn't catch fire as Marie turned off the lights in the room and lit the sparklers.

In the dark afternoon, the tree glimmered joyfully while they sang. Marie opened the door to the porch. "Now!" she called, and while singing as loudly as they could along with the CD player, *"Nu är glada julen slut, slut, slut,"* they heaved the sparkling tree into the backyard. A few people armed with streamers blew them across the room; others honked tiny paper noisemakers. Lena made a wreath of streamers and placed it on Calista's head.

"Långdans," Marie called through the ruckus.

Calista looked questioningly at Lena.

"Long dance," Lena translated.

Everyone grabbed hands and formed a circle. Calista found herself between Lena and Mattias. Accompanied by loud Christmas music from the CD player, the circle opened and Marie took the lead, pulling the rest of them behind in a crazy dance through the house. Up and down the stairs they went, around the basement, through all the bedrooms, and back down into the living room.

When the dance was over, Calista was breathing hard. "Interesting custom," she said to Mattias, letting go of his hand. "I can't see a bunch of American teenagers doing this on their own."

Lena and Mattias laughed.

"You're not gonna tell my friends, are you?" Mattias asked. "It's not really that cool here either, at least not if you're over eight or under thirty-five."

"I promise," Calista said, laughing. They were moving to the hallway, where people had begun putting their coats and shoes back on.

"Do you want to do something together sometime?" Mattias asked.

Calista was a bit taken aback, since she had only

just met him. Lena was moving out the door, but Calista caught Monique's eyes and saw her nodding slightly. Had Monique set her up with Mattias? Monique and Cory were watching them and seemed to be waiting for Calista's reply.

"Sure," Calista said, at last. "As a matter of fact, I was planning to go see the Viking exhibit at the Historical Museum soon. Maybe we could go together?"

"Okay," Mattias said. "That sounds...great."

Calista gave Mattias her phone number. Nothing wrong with getting to know someone a little better, and if he was friends with Monique and Cory, Calista thought, she'd probably like him, too. Besides, she didn't want to disappoint Monique if she had gone out of her way to set them up. And it would be nice to have someone to explore the city with.

"Fun party, Monique!" Calista said as she was leaving with Lena.

"Swedes are good at celebrating, aren't they?" Monique said, her arm around Cory's broad shoulders.

"Definitely," Calista agreed on her way out the door. Especially when one of them asks for your number, she added silently.

A couple of weeks later, after school on a Friday, Calista was waiting on the stairs outside the Historical Museum for Mattias. They had talked a few times after Monique's party, but this was the first time they'd been able to meet.

Calista looked at her watch. Mattias was fifteen minutes late. She would just go in by herself.

"Calista!" Mattias was running toward her, up the stairs. "Sorry, I got out of school late, and then I missed the train." He gave her a quick hug.

"It's okay," she said.

As soon as they had entered the building, checked their coats, and walked up the steps to the Viking exhibit, she forgot how cold she'd been while waiting outside. "How cool," Calista burst out. "Look at that."

"I know," Mattias said, sounding less than enthusiastic. "I've been here before."

They were approaching a tall black cave, the outside of which was entirely covered with phosphorescent blue runes, each probably a foot tall. The blue light from the runes also reflected off the shiny hardwood floors and gave the entire scene a dreamlike quality. Through the opening in the cave you could see a warm, shimmering light.

They walked through the opening. A small village built from sand and clay sat in a large glass case in the middle of the room.

"Look," Calista said again, reading a sign. "It says here that life was so hard that more than half of the children of this era died before age ten. Can you imagine?"

"Mm-hmm," Mattias said.

"Now this is what I really wanted to find out more about," Calista said, walking up to a rune stone by the back wall. Calista read aloud. "It says that they carved runes into all kinds of things, like combs and pieces of wood, but that most of those things are gone now. Here's an amulet with a spell carved into it in runes—someone was trying to protect himself from his enemies."

Mattias didn't respond.

Calista turned to him. "You don't exactly love this museum, do you?" she asked finally.

"Oh, I don't mind," he said.

Calista sighed. She was walking around this incredibly exciting place with someone who "didn't mind." That wasn't exactly her idea of a great first date. But moving around the exhibit, she soon forgot about Mattias and became more and more convinced that she had picked the perfect time period for her project.

One plaque in particular grabbed her attention. She read the information, then turned toward Mattias excitedly. "There never really were a people called the Vikings! That term is something historians in the late 1800s made up for all the different people who lived during that time period. Did you know that?"

"I guess," Mattias said. He obviously wasn't interested in discussing the exhibit, so Calista took her cues from him and they went on to talk about the upcoming soccer spring training, a topic they stayed on until they had walked through the rest of the exhibit and it was time to go home.

"I'll call you," Mattias said as they got their coats and backpacks from the coatroom. "Let's go see a movie sometime."

Calista nodded. "Okay," she said, and gave him a quick hug good-bye. She realized that she wasn't completely sure about seeing him again, but he was a nice enough guy, and she figured it couldn't hurt. At least she knew her dad would be excited to know about the soccer conversation they'd had. And maybe they'd really hit it off on their second date. She remembered her first date with Jonas, and how she'd recapped their soccer talk with Dad later. Some things, she realized, were the same even when she was in Sweden and thousands of miles from home.

Chapter Six

As the weeks passed by, the light began returning to central Sweden. It was getting easier to get up in the morning, and it was no longer dark when Calista walked to the train after school. Still, mornings, especially Friday mornings, were not Calista's favorite time of day. She tried to wake up enough to listen to what Ripan was saying in philosophy class.

As usual, Ripan was battling the chalk. A cloud of dust gathered around her shoulders, and her dress had chalk marks all over the front.

On the board she had written:

a) control self-interest for advantage of most
b) all persons are equal

"What are ethics?" Ripan asked, thoughtfully cocking her head to one side.

"Choosing between good and bad," someone in the back row said.

"Very well," Ripan said. "What is 'good'?" She called on Amalia, who was sitting next to Calista.

"Something that adheres to the moral codes of society," Amalia said.

"Not bad," Ripan said. "Which society?"

Lena pushed her notebook in front of Calista. *"Vill du hänga med på fika söndag eftermiddag?"* Calista glanced at her calendar. Could she go out for *fika*—a term Swedes used to mean coffee and something sweet to eat—on Sunday afternoon?

"So, how do you decide on moral codes and ethics, and who decides what's good?" Ripan asked, hitting her chalk against the board.

Nobody raised a hand.

"Class is over, but I want you to think about it," Ripan said. "It's a big question."

Calista sighed. A huge question was more like it. As she packed her book bag, she turned to Lena. "I can't go for *fika*. Britta's making waffles for *Marie Bebådelsedag*, which is Annunciation Day, I think. Do you want to come

over? She invited our neighbors, too, Karin and Moa."

"Okay," Lena said. "I'll come. But what's Annunciation Day? My family hasn't ever celebrated it. I don't understand it in either language."

"Me neither. Let's ask Bengt. He loves to talk about Swedish history. It'll be like giving him a present."

The house was filled with the welcoming smell of newly baked waffles by the time Lena arrived at the Öhströms' house on Sunday afternoon. Calista greeted her at the door, then led the way to the kitchen and a stack of waffles.

"Hey, no stealing," Britta said, raising her spatula like a weapon to protect the waffles.

"Okay, okay." Calista laughed. "I guess I'll have to wait."

"*Hej,* Lena," Britta said. "Nice to see you again. Why don't you two set the table?"

Chatting, the girls set out plates and silverware. They finished just as Bengt came home from a walk. Someone rang the doorbell right behind him. Karin, Moa, and... Håkan, stepped into the small entryway.

"Hi," Håkan said to Calista when the other two had moved into the dining room. "How are you?" he asked in Swedish.

"Fine," she answered. To her embarrassment, she found that she was blushing again. Why did Håkan have this effect on her?

They all made their way into the dining room, and

somehow Calista ended up sitting next to Håkan. Lena, who was sitting across from her, quickly struck up a conversation with Karin about the different qualities of wool yarn. Apparently, Karin was a felter and a quilter. Moa was sitting next to Lena, picking at her short fingernails, her face sporting its usual wet-blanket look.

Britta started passing around a plate piled high with waffles, and Bengt passed a glass bowl full of whipped cream and a porcelain pot with warm strawberry jam. As Moa passed the whipped cream across the table to Håkan, she smiled and said something to him in Swedish that Calista didn't catch.

They are such an odd couple, Calista thought. "How long have you two been going out?" she blurted out to Håkan while putting much too large a pile of waffles on her plate. She sucked in a quick breath. Oh, no. She couldn't believe she had asked that. It was none of her business. There was something about being around Håkan that made her say stupid things.

"The two of who?" Håkan looked confused.

Then it struck her. Oh, God! It should have been so clear. They *weren't* going out! This time Calista blushed hard, her ears heating to boiling.

"Moa and I are friends," Håkan said. He continued quietly, "We've known each other since we were in diapers. I guess I can see why you'd think we were a couple since we hang out so much."

Calista had no idea what to say. She glanced at Lena, who seemed to notice that she was struggling.

Lena bit the bottom of her lip as though she were thinking. "Hey, Cal, remember, we have a question for Bengt," she said at last. Calista sent her a grateful look. "What is *Marie Bebådelsedag*, and why do we eat waffles on this holiday?" Lena continued. "Calista told me you're into history. She thought you might know."

Bengt thoughtfully raised his knife in the air. Calista had seen him do this before. It meant he was about to talk at great length about something he enjoyed. You could tell by the way his eyes glittered that he loved when people asked him questions he could answer.

"During the time when our country was Catholic," he said, "Annunciation Day, the day when the angel Gabriel appeared to Mary telling her she would have a baby, was called *Vårfrudagen*. That would translate to something like Lady Spring Day," he added, turning to Calista. "I know your Swedish is good, but that's a tough one."

Calista smiled and nodded.

"Anyway," he continued, "in some parts of the country, local dialects made people call *Vårfrudagen*, '*våfferdagen*.' It was just a pronunciation mistake. Because the mispronunciation sounded like *våffeldagen*, or 'Waffle Day,' the tradition grew to celebrate the day by eating waffles.... How is that for a profound spiritual reason for eating waffles?"

Everyone, including Calista, laughed out loud. Then, just as she was about to take another bite of waffle, a big glob of whipped cream and strawberry jam dropped onto her white sweater.

Calista dabbed at it with her napkin, spreading the pink goo over the material. "Shit," she whispered under her breath. Håkan dipped his napkin in his glass of water and started dabbing, too. He did manage to get some of it off, but having Håkan dab away at the front of her sweater like that was unsettling. They exchanged an awkward look.

"It's okay," Calista said, standing up. She was not going to blush one more time. "I'll just change. Then I can put the sweater in water."

When Calista returned downstairs, the rest of the group was having coffee in the living room. Håkan made room for her on the couch as they all continued chatting. Even after two whole months in Sweden, Calista still got exhausted from translating, speaking, and hearing Swedish all day, and now she felt the familiar fog taking over her brain. Still, she enjoyed sitting next to Håkan, hearing everyone talk without really listening to what they were saying. Håkan's body was warm, and he smelled nice. She was sorry when Karin and Moa stood up to leave, and Håkan got up to go with them.

Exhausted, but not yet ready to go to bed, Calista logged on for a quick message to Sammie and Leah. She should send a short e-mail to Suzanne as well, she

thought, even though she knew she'd probably get snippy
comments in return.

Från: Calista@email.com

Till: Sammiesam@email.com, leahwinter@email.com

Ämne: Waffle Day

Sammie, Leah, hi,

Today is Waffle Day in Sweden. Our neighbors Karin
and Moa came over with Moa's friend Håkan. Håkan looks
so much like the Swedish prince, Carl Philip, it's creepy.
He has shaggy brown hair that curls under his ears and
really intense brown eyes, and when you talk to him, he
really listens.

Oh, and I've gone out with this guy, Mattias, a couple
times. I met him at a party a while ago. My friend Monique
set us up. He's sweet and he's cute, and e-mails a lot, but
we'll see what happens.

Anyway, I just wanted to let you know that I'm over
Jonas—the jerk—and wanted to thank you both for being
such good friends. Even though I don't write that often, I
miss you guys.

XO

Cal

After she pushed the send button, she took a deep breath.
She needed to e-mail Suzanne. She was her twin sister

after all, and it had been weeks since Suzanne had e-mailed about Jonas. But for some reason, Calista didn't know what to write besides "How's piano practice?" Why did communicating with Suzanne seem so hard? Cal wasn't really mad at her twin for anything. It was just that it had been so long since they'd *really* talked. The least she could do was e-mail her, she decided.

Från: Calista@email.com

Till: Suzic@email.com

Ämne: Jonas

Suzanne, Hi, How're things?

So, I'm sorry I didn't tell you about Jonas before. There isn't much to talk about, actually. He said that he didn't have time for a girlfriend right now. Pretty rotten, but I'm okay. I've seen another guy a few times, and I have cool friends here.

I guess it's time to start crossing my fingers for your audition. You must be getting excited.

Good luck in the Big Apple in a few weeks.

Cheers,

Cal

The following morning Calista checked her e-mail before going downstairs for breakfast. She had a note back from Sammie.

Från: Sammiesam@email.com
Till: Calista@email.com
Ämne: Hej!

Hej, Cal (is that how you say hello?),

Håkan sounds cute. Leah showed me a picture of Prince Carl Philip. He's hot! But what about that other guy, Mattias? I guess I'm a little confused.

OMG, guess what, Cal? Leah and I ran into Jeff Baker at Econoshop. He works there as a bagger. Let's just say he hasn't been taking care of himself. I guess he played football for the U of M for one season. Then he got sick of school, and the football thing didn't pan out. One tiny little question for you, Cal—WHAT DID YOU EVER SEE IN THAT GUY??? He might be good-looking (used to be at least), and he was probably an okay football player, but Cal, seriously, there is nothing in there!

Your mom and dad got a huge pottery order from this fancy restaurant in the Twin Cities, and now we're all working around the clock. Yay. ☹

Luv + miss ya,

Sammie

Calista sighed and quickly typed out a reply to Sammie's e-mail.

Från: Calista@email.com
Till: Sammiesam@email.com
Ämne: Jeff Baker

I went out with the guy like, two years ago, Sammie. How am I supposed to remember what I saw in him? He wasn't so bad. We had fun. I don't know that you're a reliable boyfriend judge, anyway. Remember your boyfriend, Fred something…All he ever did was play those weird magic card games.

Glad you are there to help glaze pottery. Rather you than me. Now I have to get back to my exotic Swedish life (wink, wink).

Cal (who doesn't want to be reminded of any more old boyfriends)

School felt slower than usual that morning. Outside the window it was starting to snow, but it looked more like rain—heavy, wet, fluffy drops. Calista's tennis shoes were still wet from her walk from the train. In the front of the room, the French teacher was jabbering away, but Calista had a hard time listening. She was still thinking about what she had liked about Jeff Baker. She remembered talking to her dad about his football games, but that's all that came to mind.

"Gamla Stan? Lunch?" Lena whispered.

Calista smiled. That was the nice thing about Lena. They often seemed to be in the same mood, knowing each other's thoughts. That's how it used to be with Suzanne, Calista remembered. They used not even to have to talk to know what the other one was thinking. But now she could barely think about what to write to her in a short e-mail. When had that all changed?

Calista shrugged off the memory and nodded to Lena. "Do we have time? Is it far?"

"Not too far, and we'll make time. Monique is coming."

Yes, it would be nice to get out of this stuffy building, Calista thought. It must be midsemester blues.

The girls made footprints in the slush as they walked out on Drottninggatan, the street outside Klara Norra Gymnasium. Instead of turning toward the used-book stores and antiques stores, they turned toward Kungsgatan, the major avenue connecting the island of Kungsholmen with the ritzy part of town called Östermalm.

Drottninggatan wasn't open to car traffic there, and they could walk in the middle of the street between rows of stores, restaurants, and movie theaters.

Soon, the girls crossed a bridge and found themselves in a courtyard.

"These buildings house the Swedish Parliament," Lena said. She motioned toward the pale yellow multistory buildings on both sides of them. "The Parliament has its own island."

"That's nice," Monique said, her voice irritated, "but these cobblestones suck." Her high-heeled boot had gotten stuck in a crack. "Could they bring it up to the twenty-first century already? Haven't they heard of asphalt?" She grinned at Lena and Calista.

Lena laughed. "I don't think high-heeled boots were on their minds a few hundred years ago when they made this street."

"This is amazing," Calista said, turning. "There are bridges everywhere."

"Yeah, Stockholm is built on fourteen islands," Lena said. "Fifty-seven bridges connect them. Six bridges lead to Gamla Stan, which is the oldest commercial part of Stockholm. Incredible, isn't it?"

Calista laughed. "You're starting to sound like Bengt," she told Lena.

The buildings of Gamla Stan stood so close together that walking into the old town felt a little like walking into a maze. They followed a small winding cobblestone street, Västerlånggatan, famous for its boutiques, candy stores, and coffee shops. Calista felt as though she had entered a movie set. She was surrounded by architecture that was hundreds of years old. The five- or six-story buildings around her looked like they were cut from an architecture magazine.

"Look!" Calista called out. "This is amazing."

Monique took Calista's camera and snapped pictures

of Lena and Calista reaching their arms out in the alley, almost touching the walls of the buildings on both sides of them.

"These alleys were clearly not built for cars," Calista said.

"Would you believe that people living in the apartments above us would just open their window and empty their bedpans in the street," Lena said. "Imagine the stench."

"Ick," Monique said. "How disgusting!"

Lena pulled them down a side street. They stopped in front of a tiny restaurant. A sign above the entrance said HERMITAGE. Even inside, the building looked historic. Calista couldn't stop staring at everything around her, including the huge buffet. Lena explained that it was a vegetarian restaurant, and that it was popular with locals because it was inexpensive and had so many menu options.

Calista took a lunch tray and started helping herself to food from the buffet table. Soon, she had a few pieces of hard bread with butter and cheese, a bowl with carrot salad, some rustic bread, hummus, and a garlicky-smelling lentil soup. She reached into her pocket for a *tiokronors* coin when...*Snap!*

"Monique!" she said with an embarrassed smile. Monique continued snapping pictures of everything.

The guy at the counter who was taking her money laughed good-naturedly. "Tourists?" he asked them in English.

Calista nodded apologetically and pointed at Monique. "*She* is. I'm here to study."

Monique laughed and waved at the guy, who happened to have a killer smile and adorable dimples.

Even after they sat down, Monique made several trips back to the counter for napkins, another glass of water, a few more garbanzo beans.

"What's going on, Monique?" Calista finally asked. "Do you have a crush on the cashier?"

"*Look* at him," Monique said, grinning. "He's hot."

Calista agreed. "But what about Cory?"

"What *about* Cory? We're just dating."

"Oh," Calista said. "I guess I'm 'just dating' Mattias, too."

"He really likes you, you know," Monique said. "He told Cory."

"I was afraid of that," Calista said. "We've only gone out a couple times, but he e-mails a lot. I'm not sure how I feel about him, though."

"Well, you don't have to know for sure. There isn't anything wrong with dating." Monique dug into her carrot salad.

"I know," Calista said, her voice thin. "But you should like the guy you're dating, right?" She sighed. "I don't know what I really want. Thinking about Mattias gives me these flashbacks to when I went out with Jonas, and now I keep wondering what I ever saw in him. I liked the fact

that he was a soccer player and that my dad could relate to him, and a part of me enjoyed the fact that Suzanne could never land such a hot guy, but I can't believe those were the only reasons."

"What's wrong with that?" Monique asked. "I don't have much reason to date guys, other than the fact that they're cute, and it's a fun distraction."

"Cal, have you ever thought about why you agreed to go out with both of them in the first place?" Lena asked thoughtfully. "It sounds like you dated Jonas in part because you knew your dad would like him—"

"And I'm the one who set you up with Mattias," Monique admitted, interrupting Lena.

"That's true," Calista agreed. "That may have been what started the relationships, but I was definitely interested in Jonas and Mattias when I first met them. They're both hot!"

Monique and Lena laughed. "But that shouldn't be the only reason you keep dating a guy," Lena said. "Did you have things in common with Jonas or Mattias?"

"Not much," Cal realized out loud. She put her knife and fork down. She wasn't hungry anymore. In fact, she had a stomachache.

"Hey," Monique said encouragingly, "all you need now is to find a cute boy that you actually have something to talk about with!"

"Sure, sounds simple," Calista deadpanned. She sighed

and slowly stood from the table. The girls carried their trays to a tray holder in the corner of the restaurant before stepping out the door.

"Cal, what about Håkan?" Lena perked up suddenly as they stepped outside. "He's cute, and you obviously have a lot in common. Both times I've seen you two together you talked to each other nonstop."

"Håkan?" Monique asked. "Who's he?"

"Just a friend," Calista said, but she found that she was blushing. Again.

As usual, Lena seemed to read Calista's discomfort. "I am so not ready to go back to school," she said, obviously trying to lighten the mood. "Let's skip our next class and go to Gallerian. I need to pick up a computer game for my niece for her birthday."

Calista shivered involuntarily. The game store in Gallerian was where Håkan worked! Did Lena know that? Was she trying to set her up with Håkan? How was that any different from Monique setting her up with Mattias? She felt like a sailboat blowing about on a stormy sea, being tossed every which way. But she didn't want to go back to school either, and since she couldn't articulate a single other reason not to go to Gallerian, she soon found herself between Lena and Monique, trekking through the slush toward the shopping center.

The game store was situated on the top floor at the far

end of a glitzy, indoor shopping mall. On their way up the escalator, the don't-do-it voice in Calista's head got increasingly louder. "Maybe you should go alone after school, Lena," she said.

Lena put her arm through Calista's and pulled her gently toward the store. "I don't have time to go later."

A *bing* sounded as they walked through the open glass doors. Calista's heart jumped when she noticed Håkan in the back of the store. His hair was tousled in the back, in a way that made her want to go up and smooth it. She had almost forgotten how cute he was. He was so engrossed in helping someone he didn't even turn to look when they walked in.

Håkan took a box from the wall and opened it. The kid he was helping, who was around twelve or thirteen and wearing a ripped leather jacket, was paying close attention to what Håkan was showing him.

When she moved to the side, Calista could see behind the console in the middle of the room to the checkout counter. On top of the counter, her legs covering the entire surface, only her combat boots dangling over the edge, sat Moa, playing a handheld video game.

"Hey, let's go," Calista whispered to Lena, pulling at her arm. She couldn't stand the thought of having Moa think she had come to the store just to see Håkan. But it was too late. Moa had already seen them. She did that little tilt of her head, then returned to her game.

Lena pulled Calista toward the computer games along one wall. "I'm just buying a game, Cal. It's no big deal. Relax."

At the back of the store, Håkan took down one more box, then another. He glanced at Monique.

"I'll be with you in a minute," he called. "Let me know if you need help with anything."

Finally the boy must have decided he wasn't going to buy anything. He said thank you and left. Håkan walked up to Monique.

"Is there anything I can help you find?" he asked. Calista was grateful he seemed only polite, not flirty, talking to Monique. Though why should she care?

Monique pointed in Calista's direction. Håkan turned. A wide smile spread on his face.

"*Hej*, Cal. What are you doing here? Moa, Cal's here," he called toward the checkout counter, as though Moa would actually think this was good news. No answer. He walked up to Calista. "I've been hoping you'd come by."

"Lena needs a game for her niece," Calista said, out of breath.

Håkan looked at his watch. "Don't you have class?"

"Hey"—Monique laughed—"no fair. Do you ask everybody that? Like the chick on the counter?"

"I guess not." Håkan smiled. Moa looked up. She didn't look like she much cared to be called a chick, but she quickly bent over her game again.

Håkan showed them around the store.

"We'd better get back to class," Calista said finally, after Lena had picked something out for her niece and paid at the counter, now vacated by Moa.

Håkan touched Calista's shoulder casually. "I'm glad you stopped by. Next time, come during lunch and I'll take you out for coffee."

"Uh, yeah…that would be nice," Calista stammered, thinking it wasn't an invitation, just something you said. It didn't really mean anything.

Monique and Lena seemed to be trading conspiratorial smirks about Håkan, but Calista was grateful that neither of them mentioned him on the way out of the mall. The girls walked through the underground tunnel to Sergels Torg, where they soon emerged on the open plaza at the bottom of an enormous staircase. A tall glass pillar statue dominated the plaza. A little old lady in a fur coat was sitting on a bench, singing and playing a keyboard. It made Calista remember Suzanne. "My sister, Suzanne, had her audition at Juilliard today. It's this really fancy music school in New York City, probably the best in the States. Cross your fingers that she got in. It's a matter of life and death for her." *I probably should have called to wish her luck,* Calista thought with a twinge of guilt.

"From everything you've told me about her, it sounds

like she'd get in with her hands tied behind her back," Lena said.

"Probably."

A few minutes later the girls were back in class, Lena in fiber arts, and Monique and Calista in Swedish culture. Calista continued to work on her Viking project, but she had a hard time focusing. For some reason, she couldn't get the feel of Håkan's hand on her shoulder out of her mind.

At supper that night Calista told Bengt and Britta about running into Håkan and Moa at Gallerian, and about Suzanne's big audition. They had almost finished eating when Britta asked how Lena was. Calista remembered that she still hadn't mentioned the trip to Lena's cabin to Bengt and Britta. Lena had invited her when Calista had dinner at her house, and the girls had since decided they'd go this weekend.

"I would like to go with Lena to her parents' cabin this weekend," she said. Then she added, "Is that okay? Her parents aren't going. It would be just the two of us."

Britta laughed. "Of course it's okay."

Swedes seemed to be pretty relaxed about letting their kids go places alone, Calista thought. In this case, that was a good thing.

Calista spent a long time at the supper table that night, chatting with Bengt and Britta, intentionally putting off the

unpleasant thing she had finally decided she had to do.

By the time they got up from the table, the evening news was on in the living room. She had to do it, she thought, no more procrastination.

She went upstairs and, resolutely, dialed Mattias's number. "Mattias," she said as soon as she heard his voice on the phone. She had planned to make small talk first, but now she knew she just had to say it. "I can't go out with you anymore, Mattias. I'm sorry. You're a cool guy, but this just isn't right for me."

Mattias was quiet for a few moments. Then he said, "I guess I knew this was coming. We don't have much to talk about, do we?"

Calista felt relieved. "We don't. But I like you, Mattias. And it has been fun spending time with you."

When she pushed the off button after they'd said their good-byes, Calista was filled with relief. Still, an irritating thought was nagging in the back of her mind. She knew now that she had gone out with Mattias because Monique had set them up, and she hadn't wanted to disappoint her. And she had figured out that she had gone out with Jonas, not only because he was fun, and cute, and because her dad liked his athletic ability, but also because Sammie thought she should. She shivered. Was she living her life according to what other people thought she should do?

When Jonas had suggested she come to Sweden for a visit, she threw herself into the language and culture full force. Yes, it had turned out that she loved it, but her reasons for coming to Sweden to study abroad bothered her. Had she no free will? Should she question every decision she thought she'd made? And if she did, where would that leave her?

"Calista, telephone for you," Britta called the following morning, her voice still groggy with sleep.

Calista rubbed her eyes and checked her alarm clock. Six A.M. Who would call this early? she wondered. Then she remembered—Suzanne must have returned from New York and her audition. It must be, what, eleven P.M. their time? She reached for the phone.

"Cal!"

Calista knew immediately from the tone of Suzanne's voice that something was wrong.

"Suze, what is it?"

"Oh, Cal." Suzanne was sobbing at the other end. Then she said something Calista couldn't hear.

"Suzanne, I can't understand you. Did something happen to Mom or Dad?" Calista's voice was loud now.

"Mom and I just got back from New York. I totally flopped!"

Suzanne sobbed so hard Calista had to move the phone from her ear, a wave of relief washing through her. Thank God no one was hurt. Then it hit her what Suzanne had just said. She sank down on her still-warm bed.

"Oh, Suze, I'm so sorry," she said. Her eyes filled with tears. Despite their differences, Calista had wanted Suzanne to get into Juilliard. It had been Suzanne's one and only goal in life. She had been so determined. She must feel awful, losing the only thing she had ever worked for. "Are you sure?" Calista asked. "You don't have the results yet, do you?"

Suzanne sobbed. "Not everybody found out," she said. "Only those they were really sure about—like me. I don't know what happened. I froze. Everything was wrong. It was like my fingers were made of wood. I kept making mistakes and couldn't find my place, and I was off beat the whole time."

"Oh, Suzanne."

"I couldn't stop crying the entire way home on the plane." Suzanne sniffled and blew her nose. "And Dad's not even home. He's at a pottery convention. I'm so nervous about telling him. What's he going to say? He had such great hopes for me."

"Don't worry about Dad." Calista wanted to say something more, something to make Suzanne feel better, but what do you say when someone's world falls down around her shoulders? Suzanne was sniffling quietly.

"Suzanne," Calista said finally. "I'm so sorry things didn't work out with Juilliard, but you know what, I'm really glad you called me."

"Me, too," Suzanne said. Then, with her voice barely

audible, "Calista, I know we've both been busy, but I've really missed you."

Calista felt a pang of guilt. "I've missed you, too, Suze." She wiped away the tear that had made its way down her cheek.

After she said good-bye and turned off the phone, Calista lay back down on her bed. When Jonas had broken up with her, she remembered, her first thought had been to write Leah and Sammie, not Suzanne. Yet the first thing Suzanne had done when she returned from New York, devastated, was to call Calista. Though she was sad for Suzanne, Calista realized something else, that what she told Suzanne on the phone was true, she *had* missed her. In fact, she had been missing her for years. When had they started growing apart? Was it in eighth grade, when Calista first started dating and was preoccupied with boys? Or was it in ninth grade, when Suzanne started getting serious about the piano and seemed to be moving into a whole different league? And what had they been bickering about so often? Calista couldn't even remember why she'd been angry with Suzanne the night before she left for Sweden. But it didn't matter anymore, Calista told herself. That was history. From now on she would make an effort to *really* talk to Suzanne. Suzanne was her sister, her *twin* sister, and nothing should come between them.

Chapter Seven

A week had passed since Calista talked to Suzanne on the phone about Julliard. This time it was Suzanne who hadn't responded to Calista's e-mail. Though Calista wasn't really worried—Suzanne would write when she felt ready—she was relieved when she finally found a message from her in her in-box.

Från: Suzic@email.com
Till: Calista@email.com
Ämne: A date

Cal,

It's so strange, I've had so much time this past week when I haven't had to practice the piano. (You'd think I could have responded to your e-mail quicker—thank you for the message, btw.)

After school I work in the shop and glaze pottery (surprise), but I still have a ton of time. I've been reading, and hanging out with people I didn't even know I knew.

I don't feel so bad about Juilliard anymore, just confused—like "What the heck do I do now?"

I told Dad about the audition when he got back from his convention, and he was really good about it. I don't know why I expected he would think it was the end of the world. He never said anything that would make me think that.

So here's some other news. I went on a date. With Mike. I know it's not a real date when you've known someone since you were little. Mike feels more like a brother, but still. We went to the movies in Rice Lake. Sammie and Leah came, too. I hope you don't mind, Cal, that I'm borrowing your friends. They've been really nice to me at school, and I've enjoyed working in the studio and at the shop with Sammie. It's strange how they've been coming to our house all my life, and I didn't even really know them.

Leah went with Spencer, and Sammie with Connor Hansen. After the movie, we went to Culvers. It was kind of fun to go on a date, even if it was just Mike.

Mom said you're going to some cabin with Lena this
weekend. Have fun.

Ttyl,

Suze

Calista read Suzanne's e-mail one more time. She could
tell that Suzanne was making an effort to be close again,
just like Calista was. But there was something else in the
e-mail that intrigued her—what Suzanne said about Dad's
reaction when she didn't get into Juilliard. "I don't know
why I expected he would think it was the end of the world.
He never said anything to make me think that."

Calista closed her eyes. That was exactly the thought
she had had about her dad. She thought he would be
disappointed about her breakup with Jonas. But when her
parents found out about it from Suzanne, they had sent
her a supportive e-mail telling her how sorry they were.
She knew her mom would feel that way, because she
never seemed to have any expectations of her or Suzanne,
but her dad surprised her. He didn't seem the least bit
disappointed to have Jonas out of the picture. For some
reason, Calista expected him to react differently, just like
Suzanne had. It was amazing how similar—despite their
differences—she and Suzanne actually were.

When Calista walked out from Klara Norra's yard that
afternoon, it smelled like spring. Finally. In late March. The

air was fresh, and though the grass was still yellow, and the trees still bare, she heard a few birds chirping tentatively in the bushes.

Calista strolled toward the train station with a happy humming in her head. That weekend, she and Lena were going to the cabin.

As she walked, she noticed a car slowing down beside her. Her heart beat a little faster when she recognized it.

"Cal, hi!" Håkan leaned out the window of the Saab. "Wanna come for *fika* at Tintarella de Luna? It's an Italian coffee shop on Drottninggatan."

Calista nodded and crossed the street to get in beside him. Håkan seemed to have a tendency to sneak up behind her in his black Saab, a tendency she found she didn't mind.

Håkan gave her a wide grin.

"What?" she said. "Do I have something on my face?"

"No," Håkan said, still grinning. "I'm just glad to see you."

She smiled. "What are you doing here?" she asked.

"I got off work early and wanted to go out for coffee."

If coffee was all he wanted, there were plenty of coffee shops closer to where he worked. There were probably ten of them in Gallerian alone.

As though he had read her thoughts, Håkan said, "I really like the *chokladbiskvier*—a chocolate pastry—they have at Tintarella."

She should have known there was a good reason. Håkan was the kind of guy who had girls for friends, not just girlfriends. He seemed really close to Moa. And now he was making an effort to be friends with Calista.

Once they reached the coffee shop, Håkan found a parking spot and they went inside.

"So what are you up to?" Calista asked, trying to sound casual, as they found a small table by the window and sat down.

"Nothing much," Håkan said. "How have you been?"

"Fine. Lots of homework, though."

"You have Ripan, don't you?" he said. "She likes homework. Even still, her philosophy class was my favorite when I went to Klara Norra."

"What did you like about it?" Calista asked.

"It's the only class where you talk about what the point of life is," Håkan said.

"We must not have gotten to that yet," Calista replied, smiling.

Håkan laughed. "We always had interesting discussions in class. I loved talking about ethics—about the meaning of life."

"Which is…" Calista asked.

"What I took away from it—and I'm sure this is Ripan's philosophy that she indoctrinates all her poor Klara Norra students with—is that all that really matters is how we treat one another and how we get along in society. 'Community, community, community,' she used to say."

Calista nodded, thinking about it.

"Though I think it begins at home," Håkan continued. "First family, then community, then the world."

"Yeah," Calista said. "It makes sense." Family was the most important thing. How could she have let herself forget that about Suzanne and herself for so many years?

Their coffee and Håkan's *chokladbiskvi* arrived. He held it across the table for Calista to taste. Mm. Of all the things she had eaten in Sweden, this chocolaty, almondy, fluffy thing, with a chewy, crunchy bottom, had to be the most divine. She took a mouthful of coffee to go with it. "What?" Calista asked Håkan. "Why are you looking at me like that?"

"Oh, no reason," Håkan said. "I guess I just like seeing someone enjoy something as much as you do. It's like you eat with all five senses."

Calista smiled self-consciously.

"Do you want to catch a movie this weekend?" Håkan asked casually. "I'll be working at Radio Stockholm on Friday and Saturday night, but we could go on Friday afternoon."

"I can't," Calista said, wondering what it might be like to sit in a dark movie theater next to Håkan. "I'm going away with Lena. Maybe some other time."

"I'll be gone for a while after this weekend," Håkan said. "I'll be visiting my grandma in northern Sweden. Maybe I can call you when I get back?"

"Okay," Calista said.

When they had finished their coffee, Håkan drove Calista to the Öhströms' house.

Later that evening, Calista couldn't get Håkan's smile out of her mind as she packed for the trip to Lena's family's cabin. She liked Håkan, but maybe he just wanted to be friends. And maybe Calista wasn't ready to date someone new. What made Håkan so different from Jonas and Mattias? Lena's words of encouragement about Håkan—that they had a lot in common—kept coming back to her. She shrugged them off. Lena didn't know everything.

Lena's cabin was a small yellow cottage with brown trim, situated at the foot of an evergreen-covered hillock in the tiny village of Grödinge, south of Stockholm.

Lena pointed out the cabin from the road as they got off the bus. From there, it was about a quarter-mile walk to the house, along a small gravel road that cut through a farmer's field. When they arrived at the house, Lena walked ahead. On top of the stone steps she pulled a key from underneath an upside-down flowerpot.

"That wouldn't have been too hard for someone else to find." Calista laughed.

"My mom and Felix would rather a thief use the key than break a window."

"You mean it's happened?"

"A few times," Lena said. She didn't look concerned. "Probably just some kids who needed a place to sleep. They usually leave things pretty nice."

"Why do you even bother locking it, then?"

"Good question."

Lena had gotten the door open while they were talking, and they stepped inside. It was cold and smelled damp. Calista remembered to take off her shoes, but she immediately wished she had brought slippers. The wooden floors were icy cold despite the multicolored handwoven rugs covering almost every bare centimeter.

The windows had white lace curtains, just like in Lena's house in town. The furniture was simple, made from blond wood, like Swedish furniture tended to be. Most noticeable in the room were the wall hangings. Calista stepped closer to what she thought was an oil painting. It was a scene from the archipelago: gray rock with three tiny red cabins, tufts of green grass here and there, grass on the cottage roofs, a Swedish flag, and blue water all around. Up close, she noticed it wasn't a painting but a textile collage.

"Jeez, Lena, this is incredible," Calista said. "The detail work on this, I've never seen anything like it."

Lena looked amused.

Calista stared at her, her mouth half open. "You did this?"

"It's no biggie," Lena said. "I was just experimenting."

"Wow," Calista said. "What about the rest of these?" She motioned to the other wall hangings.

One piece wasn't unlike the one Felix had shown her at their house in Hässelby, with thin layers of fabric on top of one another, mostly black on the outside but with glimpses of gold and silver underneath. Another was a log-cabin quilt in green and gold.

"They're hanging here because my mom and Felix insist on hanging them, and I told them they couldn't hang them up in the house in town."

"Why?" Calista asked. "You're so talented. If I had a gift like that, I'd want to share it with the world." She thought of Suzanne playing the piano at her big spring recital and smiled.

Lena shrugged and started making a fire in the black woodstove in the middle of the living room. "Before we eat, let's go for a walk," she said, signaling that the artist discussion was over.

"Can we see some rune stones?" Calista asked.

"Why not?" Lena said. "That's the main reason we're here. Why don't we walk to the one that's next to the church? The other ones we can see later. We'll have to catch the bus to get to those."

They started down the same gravel road they had come

in on. It led to the center of the village, which consisted of only a red building and a hill, on top of which stood the church.

"Not many houses in this village, are there?" Calista asked.

"No, they're spread out over the countryside." Lena gestured toward the large red building. "This used to be the old schoolhouse. Now it serves as a community center."

"Look, there's even an ironwork rooster on top of the spire of the church," Calista said, delighted, as they came closer. The bird shone brightly in the sun, catching the light as it turned slightly in the breeze.

"They started putting roosters on top of church spires in the sixteenth century. They're a symbol of watchfulness," Lena said. "What?" she asked, noticing the smile that was tugging at the corners of Calista's mouth. "I can't help it, I get it from my mom," she added, now smiling herself. "She's a lot like Bengt. She loves historical trivia."

The girls followed a road lined with budding maple trees to the top of the hill. The graveyard surrounding the white-washed church was full of oak trees and tea-rose bushes, and the gravel paths were raked into perfect stripes.

As they walked into the churchyard, they passed through the opening in a thick stone wall.

"This is it," Lena said. "Look!"

Next to the wall stood a large flat stone, reaching almost to Calista's shoulders. Though she could tell right

away that something was carved into it, it was hard to make out the runes. Time had worn the letters down so they were almost entirely gone in places. Calista peeked at the cheat sheet that she had printed off the Internet, but she pretended to read the markings on the stone. "Farulv and Ulv and Sigsten and Gunnar, they raised this stone after Roald, their father," she said.

"Very impressive," Lena said, her mouth open. Calista held out her sheet.

Lena laughed. "Okay, so you're not quite fluent in rune yet," she said. "It's only a matter of time, I'm sure."

Calista pulled out her digital camera and shot a number of pictures of the stone.

"I hope that's for class," Lena said. "Somehow I can't see your friends in Wisconsin being too excited about twenty pictures of an old stone. By the way, is this rune stone just another grave marker?"

"Kind of," Calista said, "only I don't think Roald is buried here. This is some kind of a memorial to him. Most likely, Roald was wealthy. It was expensive to hire someone to carve runes for you."

"Hey, let's go inside the church," Lena said.

The thick wooden door of the church had a black cast-iron bolt on it, but when Calista pulled at the handle, the door opened with a loud creak.

The girls walked inside and found themselves in an anteroom.

"This is where people used to hang their weapons in the olden days," Lena whispered.

It was so quiet in the church that Lena's and Calista's steps on the large stone slabs in the entrance hall could be heard even though they were wearing tennis shoes.

"Hey, look," Lena said. She pulled a brochure from the enormous wooden table in the middle of the room. A candle was burning in an iron candleholder on the table. "It's about this church. It says that most of Grödinge Kyrka was built at the beginning of the fourteenth century."

"That's like...almost seven hundred years ago. Almost as old as the Vikings. The stone was from 1000 to 1100 sometime. It must have been here before they started building the church."

"Actually," Lena said. "It says here that they think the oldest parts of the church walls might be from the 1100s, which *could* mean it was here when the stone was raised."

The girls stepped into the church, which was simply decorated but had elaborate stained-glass windows on both sides. The wooden pews looked hard and uncomfortable. The walls of the church were plain smooth white rock.

Lena turned around to face the exit. "Check this out," she said, keeping her voice low and pointing to something hanging from a balcony above them. "This is what I wanted you to see. It's a replica of the famous *Grödingebonaden*, or

The Grödinge Tapestry. The original hangs at the Historical Museum in Stockholm, and was made from a Persian-Byzantine pattern, in the early fifteenth century. The first textile project I ever did was to embroider a picture of this tapestry for my grandmother, who was born in Grödinge. It was her father who built our cabin."

The tapestry above them was woven in dark blues and grays. A lion, an eagle, and a griffin were repeated in the pattern.

"In fact, I think this tapestry might be what inspired me to want to work with textile arts."

"Then it's an important work of art," Calista said, smiling. "It's really beautiful," she added. "It's amazing to think that it was made so long ago. I wonder who wove it."

"They don't know," Lena said. "Someone worked really hard on it, but the name didn't make it into history together with the work."

The girls walked out of the church onto the raked gravel path.

"It's just so amazing," Calista said, walking down the hill, "how there are all these really old things here, memories of the people who lived before. Maybe someone who lives here now has ancestors who helped build the church in 1100. Maybe the ancestors of the person who carved the runes still lives here. Maybe they were even *your* ancestors, if your grandma grew up here."

"Maybe," Lena said, smiling.

"And to think it would be more than three hundred years after they began building this church before Columbus even sailed for America…"

Lena nodded. "It's strange to think about."

The girls walked back toward the cabin.

"Oh, look," Lena said suddenly, moving toward the ditch next to them. She reached for a tiny yellow flower that looked like a dandelion, only smaller. "It's *tussilago*. I know they don't look like much," she said, "but in Sweden they're important because they're the first wildflowers that come up in the spring. All kids pick them."

Calista bent to pick a few flowers as well. They looked like tiny suns.

As soon as they got back to the cabin, they put the flowers in a small vase, and Lena started slicing and frying the blood pudding they had brought from the city. Calista set out lingonberry sauce and butter, hard cracker bread, and cheese with cumin seeds in it.

"I can't believe how yummy this stuff is," Calista said, pouring a generous amount of lingonberry sauce over her pudding. "If someone at home had told me I would be eating pig's blood—mixed with milk, flour, beer, and syrup—then fried to a crisp, I would never have believed him."

"You make everything seem so exotic, Calista. I've never thought of blood pudding that way before."

After lunch, Lena and Calista caught the bus to visit

and photograph Nolingestenen, and the blank stone next to it. Calista recognized it as a *mehir*, a memorial stone without a carved message. Then they continued on to see the Norrga Stone, which was interesting, not for its runes, since time had erased them almost entirely, but for its art. Carved into the stone was a slithering snake with large round eyes and a flickering tongue, and a cross, an uncommon feature for rune stones.

When they returned to the cabin, Calista was content with their accomplishments. "Thanks for taking me around today. My project is really coming together now. This was just what I needed to finish up."

"Next time I go to another country, or someplace I haven't been," Lena said, "I'm going to do it just like you, throw myself in, headfirst, and learn everything I can."

"That's a nice compliment," Calista said.

Lena smiled as she worked on dinner. She opened a can of brown beans, put them in a pot, and threw a thick slab of bacon in the frying pan. She flipped on the radio by the window.

"I love this song." Calista started dancing across the kitchen floor. "Britta plays this CD all the time." When the song ended a familiar voice came on.

"And that, my friends, was Bo Kaspers Orkester with 'Who Do We Think We Are?' Stay tuned to Radio Stockholm."

"It's Håkan," Calista said, excited. "Turn it up."

Lena laughed and turned the radio up.

"It's a good day for…hm, let's see," Håkan continued on the radio, "something slow and sensual. How about Norah Jones? Yes, Norah it is."

"You can tell he loves to DJ," Lena said. "He's got the perfect voice for it, deep and sexy."

Calista nodded. "He does have the perfect voice."

After finishing the dishes, they started a game of Scrabble, or Alfapet, as Lena called it. Calista did her best, but Håkan's voice on the radio made it difficult for her to concentrate.

"Oh, no," Calista sighed, looking at her letters. "It's impossible to do this in Swedish. I'll never be able to beat you."

She pondered the tiny letter squares in front of her, taking a mouthful of the hot chocolate Lena had made. She had a terrible mess of *å*'s, *ä*'s, and *ö*'s.

Mås, she wrote. *Lök*, the next time. Then *Älv*.

After a number of impossible six- and seven-letter words, Lena won big with the Swedish word for pea soup: *ärtsoppa*.

"I have a feeling I couldn't have beaten you even in English," Calista said.

It was late when the girls finally crawled into Lena's parents' queen-sized bed. Luckily, Håkan had gone off the air a few hours earlier. It would have been impossible for Calista to turn off the radio while he was still talking.

Suddenly, lying in the dark, listening to the silence around her, Calista remembered the weekends with her family at the small cabin by the lake. The memory of Suzanne and her in the large bed together, talking into the night, was almost overwhelming. There was nothing they hadn't told each other. Then, when their parents bought the pottery business, they had sold the cabin.

"Are you close to your sisters?" Calista asked into the dark.

Lena was quiet for a while. "Not Linn. She and I still argue. Everything she does annoys me. Sandra and I would be close if she lived here, but Belgium is so far away. I don't know much about her daily life. How about you and Suzanne?"

"Suzanne and I used to be really close. I don't know what happened. When she got serious about playing the piano, I thought she got snooty, but now I'm thinking I just might have been jealous. She's amazing at the piano, actually. She's really gifted, like you are with your tapestry."

After a short pause, Calista continued. "When she didn't get into Juilliard, she called me, really upset. I think she just wanted to hear my voice. I remembered what it used to be like, talking to her about everything."

"Do you think it can be like that again?"

"I don't know. I guess I'll have to keep trying and wait and see." Somehow, though, being there with Lena made Calista feel hopeful, like anything was possible.

Chapter Eight

After the visit to Lena's family cabin, Calista worked almost feverishly on her Swedish culture project. Never had she thought history could be this interesting.

"What do you think of this one?" Monique asked Calista in class a few weeks later. "Too psychedelic?" She had made finger-sized paper dolls for which she was designing clothes from the 1960s. She held up a miniature purple-and-orange scarf.

"It's just right," Calista said. "You should be a fashion designer, Monique."

Calista bent over her own project, which still looked

only like an enormous piece of Styrofoam. She frowned. How picky should she be about the runes? she wondered. The alphabet changed over the 350 years she was covering, A.D. 750 until around A.D. 1100, and it varied in different parts of the territory. Which runes should she use?

In the front of the room Kathy was helping one of the students put together a PowerPoint presentation on the mining strikes in northern Sweden at the beginning of the twentieth century. In one corner, two other students were creating a minimodel of the siege of the fortress of Fredrikshald in Norway: King Carl XII on his horse in the middle of the battling troops, just moments before he was, presumably, killed with a bullet shaped like a button.

When had she last devoted this much time to a project at home? Calista wondered. Learning about Swedish culture made her eager to learn more about American history as well. Who were the Native American tribes living in America during the time of the Vikings, and what were their cultures like? That would make an interesting project. Maybe next year's history teacher would let her delve into that.

Monique poked her with her elbow. "Class is over, Cal. In case you hadn't noticed."

Calista pulled herself out of her reverie, cleaned up her project, and headed for body balance.

After school, Calista, Monique, and Lena walked to

Hötorgshallen, the vast indoor market in central Stockholm. Calista could never get enough of the smells: the spice counter with spices from foreign lands she hadn't even heard of; the counters with cheeses, hot Moroccan sausages, beautiful colored vegetables, homemade candy, chocolate, bulk coffee. She breathed it all in.

"I'll have a double espresso," Monique said, with a wink to the young man behind the counter. She gathered her hair in a bushy ponytail.

"I think I'll have a *sockerdricka*," Calista said. "I can't see how you can drink double espresso, Monique. Don't you get ulcers?"

"Maybe, but it's worth it!" She glanced over her shoulder and smiled at the coffee guy. The girls made their way to a table and sat down. "Hey, I have an idea," Monique said. "Why don't you guys come to Uppsala with me to celebrate *Valborg* next weekend? We can stay in Marie's friend Ingrid's dorm room."

"*Valborg?*" Calista asked.

"It's the big celebration to welcome spring," Monique started. "Marie said it's superfun. Everyone gets together to party, eat, drink, sing songs, have bonfires...."

Monique looked at Lena with raised eyebrows. "Can you explain it better?" she asked.

Lena smiled. "Before I met you guys I never even thought about why we celebrated all these strange holidays. I only found out why we celebrate *Valborg* last year because my

brother, Niklas, wanted to explain it to some Israeli friends, and he wrote home and asked Mom about it. This seems to be the deal, though there are other theories: in the pre-Christian days, people used to let their animals out to pasture on the first day of May, and they wanted to make sure the woods and fields were safe for the animals. They used to gather and light huge bonfires the night before to scare away predators and possibly witches."

Calista laughed. "I love how complex this country is. I thought I would learn the language and the culture in no time, but I am more and more convinced that all I'll be able to do in one semester is scrape the surface."

"I agree," Monique said, "which is why I want to do as much as possible while I'm here. So, will you two come?"

"Of course," Calista said excitedly. Lena nodded in agreement.

The man behind the counter brought them their drinks, his eyes lingering on Monique just a moment too long.

"You guys can bring dates if you want to," Monique said, oblivious to the attention she was getting. "I'm bringing Jens, the guy with dimples from the vegetarian restaurant in Gamla Stan."

Calista gave her a questioning glance.

"Cory and I broke up. I have hope for Jens, though," Monique said. "Calista, why don't you bring Håkan?"

Calista shook her head. "Monique, I'm not going out with Håkan. He's—"

"Just a friend," Monique said. "I know."

Lena and Calista laughed.

"Don't worry about it, Cal. I don't have a date either," Lena said. "By the way, Cal, did you know that Uppsala is Viking haven? We should go visit some of the Viking sites, like the famous burial mounds, when we're there."

"I'd love to," Calista said.

As they gathered their backpacks and coats, Monique fired off a last blinding smile in the direction of the guy who had served them. "On second thought, Jens may not last long," she whispered to Calista and Lena as they walked out of Hötorgshallen, laughing.

When Calista got home, she had an e-mail from Suzanne in her in-box.

Från: Suzic@email.com
Till: Calista@email.com
Ämne: Mike

Cal,

I'm so glad we've been talking more, because I have news. Are you sitting down? Promise me you won't laugh! I am totally, recklessly, insanely in love with Mike. Are you shocked? I've known it for a while, but it was difficult to tell you for some reason. It's funny, but I keep wanting you to come home so you can meet him, forgetting that you

already know him. That's how new and strange everything feels. How can I have hung out with this guy all my life and never noticed how totally amazing he is?

You have to write me back right away, Cal, and tell me you're not laughing.

Lv,

Suze

Från: Calista@email.com
Till: Suzic@email.com
Ämne: Mike

Suzanne,

How could you think I would laugh at you? Did I ever? (Don't answer that.) I *love* it that you and Mike are going out. Mike is great, better than any guy I ever dated. I'm not *that* surprised, though, at least not as surprised as you seem to be. It's always been obvious to me that Mike liked you. I even told you once and you laughed. You were probably too busy with your piano to notice him.

Say hi to him for me. It *is* a little funny to think of the two of you as a couple, but nice funny, not weird funny.

I'm going to Uppsala next weekend to celebrate this huge festival, so I'll e-mail you later.

Love ya,

Cal

The last weekend of April arrived with sun and warm spring breezes. Calista was enjoying the weather Saturday morning as she waited on the train platform for her friends to join her for the trip to Uppsala and their *Valborg* celebrations.

"Over here," Calista hollered when she noticed Lena down the platform.

"Ready to go?" said Monique as she approached with Marie and a guy whom Calista recognized as the cashier from the vegetarian restaurant.

"This is Jens," Monique introduced.

Calista and Lena both shook Jens's hand.

Jens nodded and smiled. Calista remembered his smile, and how much time Monique had spent at the cash register talking to him that afternoon a few weeks ago.

The five of them had barely set foot on the train before it started shaking down the tracks. Calista leaned toward the window until they had left the city behind. The landscape was beautiful, hilly and green, and dotted with red houses. "Why are so many of the barns and houses painted in exactly the same color red?" she asked.

"I have no idea," Jens said.

Lena smiled. "Sweden is probably the only country in the world that actually has a national paint," she said. "Have you heard the term *Falu Rödfärg*?"

Calista shook her head. "Red paint from Falun?" she translated.

"That's it," Lena said. "Just outside of Falun there is a mine that has red pigment in its bedrock. They've mined and used this pigment in paint since the sixteenth century. In the beginning, the red paint was a sign of status and money, and only wealthy people had red houses. Then it became popular, and by the nineteenth century, farmers were painting their farmhouses and their barns red as well. In the twentieth century, for a while, people got into the modern plastic- and oil-based paints, but recently, even in very modern architecture, *Falu Rödfärg* is coming back."

"Cool," Calista said. "It looks quaint and so...Swedish."

They all laughed.

Outside the train window, the sun poured down over the slowly greening landscape, and in less than forty minutes, the train slowed to a stop and they got off at the station in Uppsala.

"Åh nej," Calista said, her eyes popping at the sight of a statue of a very large and very naked troll-like man outside the station. The troll had a huge, creepy smile and was playing the violin. At the top of the statue, above the troll's head, a happy couple was dancing away as though they hadn't a care in the world.

"That troll needs some underwear," Monique said.

Jens started laughing.

"I know," Marie said. "There's always some conservative group working to get rid of that guy, or at least cover him up. But he's been around for a long time. Art's sacred in

Uppsala, and Bror Hjort, the artist, is from here. People are pretty proud of him. The name of the sculpture is *The Reel of the Neck.*" She turned to Calista and Monique. "I don't think you have the Neck as a mythological figure in the United States. It's a naked man with long hair, playing an instrument, usually the violin, in a river, luring people into the water. He's sort of like a male siren. People say that this particular Neck looks an awful lot like Bror Hjort himself."

Calista smiled. Uppsala was an interesting town already.

The group made their way to the bus stop outside of the station and boarded a bus to Studentstaden, where they'd be staying with Marie's friend Ingrid in her dorm. As the bus wound its way around downtown Uppsala, Calista caught sight of an enormous cathedral surrounded by beautifully groomed grounds. She pulled at Lena's sleeve.

"Let's get off and look at the cathedral," she said. "It looks incredible."

Marie laughed. "We'll sightsee soon enough. Let's drop our stuff off first."

At Studentstaden, Calista and Lena offered to sleep in the third-floor common room, since Ingrid's room was on the small side.

"That's a good idea," Ingrid said, "but you'll want to spread your sleeping bags out now. Even though *Valborg* isn't until Monday, there will be hordes of people coming in this weekend fighting for floor space."

After they had laid their sleeping bags out, Calista, Lena, Monique, and Jens decided to board a bus to Old Uppsala to see Kungshögarna, or the Royal Mounds. Calista had read about it in a tourist brochure. It was an old pagan burial ground and a famous Viking site.

It didn't take long for the bus to drive past the farm fields and reach Kungshögarna, and for everyone to get off the bus.

From where they stood outside a cluster of red buildings, Calista could see a few hillocks, presumably the burial grounds. She was impressed by the three large mounds, which were covered with grass and situated on a ridge. She couldn't wait to learn more about how they were created and who was buried there. After a bit of coaxing, she convinced the others to join a guided tour group with her. She didn't want to miss a speck of information. They signed up at a booth and joined a group that was gathering nearby.

"Hi, I'm Mark." The guide in front of the group of tourists, of which they were now a part, couldn't have been much older than they were. He wore thick glasses and looked like he was frowning even when he smiled. He did have a small, cute nose that pointed up and made him look a bit like a puppy, though, which softened his otherwise austere look. "I'll be your guide today. Please let me know if you have any questions at any time."

Lena was fanning herself with a small brochure they

had received when they joined the tour. Glancing toward the guide, she pulled her sweater over her head. She wore a pale blue T-shirt underneath, which, Calista noticed, matched her eyes perfectly.

Lena was right. It was getting warm. Calista could almost hear the grass turning green around them.

"Here in Old Uppsala," Mark said, "you are walking on sacred ground with every step." He gestured behind him, toward the mounds. "People come here for the Royal Mounds, but there used to be two thousand to three thousand other mounds in this area. People have been buried here for two thousand years, ever since the area rose above sea level."

"Really?" Lena said, awe in her voice.

Calista poked her with her elbow. "*Really*, Lena," she whispered, grinning.

"Many people feel differently," Mark went on, "but I think it's a crime to dig up the old burial sites and convert them into farmland. In fact, I don't think you should dig up the old burial sites up for anything, not even in the name of science and archaeology."

Lena nodded. "Me, too," she whispered to Calista. "I've always felt that way."

"So, do we know who's buried in these graves?" Mark asked the group.

"Some old Viking kings," guessed a middle-aged woman with a short, stylish haircut.

"Now, that's what everyone believes," Mark said. "The truth is, we really don't know. The graves were here long before the people we call the Vikings. What we *do* know is that some people from the Viking age worshiped in this area and that the mounds were sacred to them. In 1846, when the East Mound, the one called Odin's Mound, was excavated, not much was found: a few burned bone fragments and some things archaeologists assumed were burial gifts."

Calista noticed that Monique and Jens were sauntering off in the direction of Odinsborg, the restaurant and café on the premises, having apparently had enough of their Swedish history lesson. Lena, on the other hand, was spellbound.

Mark started walking toward the mounds. "These mounds are often seen on the covers of books about Sweden. They date back to the fifth and sixth centuries. Can you think of a national monument older than that?"

Lena sidled up to Mark and asked him something quietly. He nodded.

Mark continued. "The bodies of the Viking-age men who may have been buried here were first burned so that the force of the fire would take them to Valhalla, the home of their gods, Thor and Odin. Like the old Egyptians, the Viking-age upper class were concerned about bringing their material goods with them to their new home, and they were buried with their riches." Mark smiled at Lena. "Greed isn't a new invention."

After walking around the mounds, Calista snapping pictures for her project all the while, Mark brought the group to the café at Odinsborg, which looked to Calista like a Viking era drinking hall, straight out of a movie. They were offered mead made from an old Viking recipe served in a Vikingesque horn. Jens and Monique, who had already tasted some, sat smirking at a table in the corner.

Calista took a mouthful from the horn Mark handed her. The sweet honey flavor, combined with a strong taste of yeast, filled her mouth and almost made her gag.

"Usch!"

"Hey," Lena said, "you even say yuck in Swedish now."

Calista laughed and handed the horn back to Mark.

"It's an acquired taste," Mark said. "The real mead makers," he continued, "are often people who are returning to the old heathenism, and they claim there are wonderful ways to spice it up. Some use a few peppercorns, some use sliced apples, and quite a few use flowers from the elder tree, as it is believed to be connected to the Nordic goddess Freya."

After a quick lunch, Calista and the rest of the group looked around in the nearby souvenir shops and museum. Lena stayed behind and chatted with Mark, her usually pale cheeks glowing bright red.

"Mark knows Ingrid," Lena called out to Monique, who was talking to Jens near a glass case full of bone fragments.

"We have a class together," Mark added.

"You should come out with us for *Valborg* on Monday," Monique said, moving closer.

Mark sent Lena a quizzical glance. Lena nodded eagerly. "That would be fun. Join us."

Before they left Kungshögarna, Lena arranged for Mark to meet the group at Ingrid's dorm on Monday morning at seven thirty, when the celebrations would begin.

"You like Mark, huh?" Calista asked on the bus back to Uppsala.

Lena nodded. "He's okay," she said, an uncharacteristic grin on her face.

"Just 'okay,'" Calista teased. "Looks to me as if you like him more than that."

Lena didn't respond, but the deep blush on her cheeks gave her away.

Calista woke on Monday morning to the sound of moving furniture. She yawned and was glad that, on Ingrid's recommendation, they had gotten to bed early the previous night after sightseeing around Uppsala.

Calista climbed out of her sleeping bag and peeked out of the common room door. In preparation for breakfast, tables and chairs had been dragged into the hallway next to the common room. Someone was draping a paper tablecloth over all the tables. Streamers were hanging from the ceiling lamps, and from the communal kitchen came the smell of boiling rice.

It was tricky to get in and out of the dorm rooms with the tables in the middle of the hallway, but everybody was genial about it. There was a buzz in the air that Calista had felt only on prom night back in Moon Lake.

At seven thirty sharp, Mark rang the buzzer to Ingrid's room and came up to join the group. Instead of his thick glasses, he was wearing contacts, which made him look almost handsome. In his hand he was carrying something that looked like a white sailor's hat.

They all found a seat at the long table, together with perhaps twenty other people, but it wasn't until they sat down that Calista noticed the champagne bottles and three large pots of what looked like gooey cooked rice.

"Champagne and rice?" Calista burst out. "For breakfast?"

The student next to her, a girl with long red hair, laughed. "Uppsala is famous for its *Valborg* champagne breakfast."

"The key to handling *Valborg*, someone told me," Lena whispered from Calista's other side, "is lots of rice porridge and very little champagne. I guess champagne has a way of sneaking up on you. One moment you're perfectly fine and then suddenly you're not."

"Thanks. I found out on New Year's that I don't care much for champagne."

The rice porridge, on the other hand, was good, cinnamon spicy, thick with cream, and full of crunchy blanched almonds.

They had just begun to eat when someone shouted, *"Lambo, hej! Lambo, hej! Tjofaderittan lambo."*

Everybody at the table, except Monique and Calista, who were sitting with their eyes wide, started singing at the same time, their glasses raised.

"You all know this song?" Calista whispered to Lena.

Lena nodded.

"What does it mean?"

"Nothing, this first part is just nonsense."

But the song started making more sense to Calista, who noticed that the singers took turns and that everybody seemed to know exactly where to join in. *"Skål,"* they called at the end of the song. Calista and Monique dutifully raised their champagne glasses and sipped. *"Skål, skål,"* everyone shouted.

The champagne breakfast lasted two hours, and the students sang almost the entire time.

"I'm so impressed that you guys know enough songs, by heart, to fill two hours," Calista said to Lena when everyone began clearing the table.

"Drinking songs are a tradition in Sweden," Lena said.

With everybody helping, the tables were cleared and the

dishes done in record time. Calista, Lena, Mark, Monique, Jens, Marie, and Ingrid got ready to go downtown.

"I've got guest IDs for you guys," Ingrid said. "So you can get into the *nationer,* which are the student clubs. You'd better take them from me now in case we get separated later.

"If we lose each other, let's meet at Norrland's Nation after the putting on of hats."

"The putting on of hats?" Calista asked. She had noticed that they were all carrying sailor's hats like the one Mark had brought.

The Swedes laughed. "It must sound strange to a foreigner," Ingrid said. "I don't think we can explain it, you'll just have to see it."

Never, not in her wildest imagination, would Calista have been able to imagine Uppsala at *Valborg.* As they approached the downtown area, the crowds were so thick on the sidewalks that people were pouring out into the streets. On every green spot in town, blankets were spread out, and people were eating pickled herring with egg salad, and drinking *nubbe*, which Lena explained was vodka with spices.

Soon, Calista found herself alone with Mark and Lena. It was difficult to keep even just three people together in the bustling crowds.

"Let's head to the river," Mark said. "You'll enjoy this."

Sure enough, long before they reached Fyrisån, the

river that ran through town, they could hear the crowd roaring from its banks.

"What is all this?" Calista asked as they neared the water.

"It's called *Forsränningen*, the Run of the Rapids," Mark said. "It's a long *Valborg* tradition in Uppsala. Students here have a reputation of being wild and playful. Years back, a group of students thought it would be a good idea to see who could build the craziest river raft, and ever since then, we've had the *'forsränning'* every year on *Valborg.*"

They pushed their way close enough to see the water. Students in costumes ranging from space uniforms to aluminum bikinis to surgical gear were traveling down the river on vessels that seemed to be put together slapdash, and looked far from seaworthy. One was made entirely of tiny margarine containers, another of something pink and foamy. Several were simple rafts carrying curious items—one featured a dining room table, on top of which was a roast on a plate, though the captain had long since fallen overboard, and was hanging on to the edge of the raft, waving to the crowd.

"How many people drown every year?" Calista asked, concerned.

Mark laughed. "It looks bad, doesn't it? But, I've never heard of anyone drowning."

Calista waved to a man in a cat suit, standing tall on a tiny raft of about one square foot, with a Swedish flag on a stick. "Do you win something at the end?" she asked.

"Not that I know of," Mark said. "Still, though, wouldn't you want to do it?"

Calista nodded and smiled. That was just what she had been thinking. On the other hand, Mark surprised her. He didn't seem like the kind of guy who would dress up in a moon suit and go down the river on a rickety raft assembled with duct tape.

After the river run, the three of them stopped at a small outdoor café for a piece of quiche—Lena had to convince Mark and Calista that they could live without the traditional lunch of *sill*, pickled herring. "I just want something normal," she protested.

Mark and Calista relented.

"So can you tell me what the sailor hat is for now?" Calista said when they had left the café and were braving the seething crowd again.

"You'll see," Mark said, and winked.

An hour later, they were fighting their way up the hill toward the university library, which was located close to Ingrid's dorm. It was packed with people standing around, waiting. Mark found a spot close to the library stairs. Calista looked around. The birds were singing in the trees around them, and Uppsala Castle shone bright red in the sunshine.

Calista noticed that everybody had their hats in their hands. "Why don't you have a hat, Lena?"

"You get it when you graduate from high school," she said.

Calista's mouth puckered into an exaggerated pout. "I won't get one? Ever? I will have to live my entire life without a cool hat like all these people have?"

Mark and Lena laughed. "That would be a correct assumption," Mark said.

"Hmmph." Calista pouted again.

Just then the crowd grew quiet. A short man with white hair walked out onto the library steps. "The dean of the university," Lena whispered.

The man raised his hand, in which he held a white hat. He was saying something in Swedish, which Calista couldn't hear. Lena explained that donning the white caps marked the change of the seasons. The man's speech ended, and he put his hat on his head. All the people, thousands of them, followed suit and put their hats on their heads as well. An enormous cry rose to the sky. Then everybody took their hats off and threw them in the air. It looked a bit like the end of a graduation ceremony. But then they caught the hats, put them back on, and started running down the library hill. It was a strange sight, all those white-hatted people, moving together like a huge, white river.

"Let's run," Calista said, grabbing Mark and Lena. They joined the crowd in a crazy spring run down the hill. When they finally reached Norrland's Nation, they were sweaty and thirsty and willingly fought the crowd by the bar.

After a round of drinks at Norrland's Nation, where Calista, Lena, and Mark, with much difficulty, found the rest of the group, they went back to the dorm room to rest.

Ingrid had not been exaggerating when she told them the dorms would be packed. There were people everywhere. Everyone in the dorm seemed to have guests for the weekend. It was, in fact, impossible to get any rest, and when it was time to start for downtown for the evening festivities, Calista was more than ready to go.

If the town had been packed earlier in the day, it was even more so now. As they walked up the hill toward the university library, Calista had the sensation that she was swimming on the sidewalk. She had the urge to grab onto Lena's hand so they wouldn't be separated, but she noticed, in the near dark, that Mark had beaten her to it.

Everywhere Calista looked, bonfires were starting to flare, lighting up the evening sky.

"This is incredible," she said as they reached the top of the hill. An amazing view of the city stretched out in the distance. "Look at the castle in the light of the bonfires," Calista said. "You can almost see the witches flying in the air."

Lena didn't answer.

"It feels unreal," Calista continued. "I'll never be able to tell people at home about this, and have them really understand."

Not even a *jaha* from Lena. Was she so wrapped up in Mark that she couldn't even answer? Calista finally turned to look at her friend. But nobody was next to her. Shoot, she'd lost everybody. She must have looked really silly talking to herself.

Despite her predicament, being all alone in this city on this strange night when anything could happen, Calista felt uplifted. There was no reason she couldn't enjoy herself even if she had lost Mark and Lena—and for all she knew, she might well find them again.

She walked toward the bonfires. It was getting very dark now, and the smell of grilled hot dogs was everywhere. Somewhere near the river a barbershop quartet was singing. The male a cappella voices sounded beautiful in the spring night. Calista walked around the castle and found the gardens Mark had told them about. Though it was early in the season for most plants, the tulips, hyacinths, and crocuses were blooming everywhere. While Calista could barely make them out in the dark, the smell was almost overpowering.

Calista walked toward an unusually large bonfire next to the gardens.

"Hej! Vill du ha varmkorv med bröd?" someone called to her. She turned to see a young woman in a white hat holding out a hot dog to her.

Calista shook her head. *"Nej tack.* Thanks for asking, though." She got a kick out of the Swedes offering you "a hot dog with a bun," like you'd ever want one without a bun!

The students around the fire looked friendly and seemed to be having a great time. When someone handed her a leaflet with song lyrics, she wondered if they thought she was a friend of someone in their group.

Calista was happy to have people to celebrate with. She squinted at the lyrics in the flickering light of the bonfire and tried to sing along. *"Vintern rasat ut i våra fjällar..."* A male voice suddenly sang out right next to her. *"Drivans blommor smälta ner och dö..."*

She moved a little to the side, but the voice followed her. She turned. In the flickering light from the fire she saw…Håkan. He was looking straight ahead, as though he hadn't seen her. She laughed and threw her arms around him. "You," she burst out. "What are the chances of that? I was wondering where you were celebrating *Valborg.*" Oh, no. Did she really say that out loud? How embarrassing. Now he'd know she'd been thinking about him.

"*Hej*, nice greeting," he said. He hugged her back but didn't let go right away. Instead they stood like that, arms around each other, for what felt like minutes but was probably only a few seconds. Calista's mind was in an upheaval. She inhaled Håkan's smell of spring evening and bonfire smoke. "So you've been thinking about me…" he said.

She let go of him. She felt weak and wobbly kneed. "Well, yeah. I was wondering how things were at your

167

grandma's." She knew it sounded lame, but she was trying to save herself from embarrassment.

Håkan smiled slyly. "Oh," he said. "I should have figured it was my grandma you were concerned about." He touched Calista's hair. "It's really strange to find you here. Almost too lucky to be true." He looked around. "Are you here by yourself?"

"I came with Lena and a guy we met touring the Royal Mounds," she said. "I seem to have lost them, though. How about you?"

"Same thing," he said. "Lucky I found you."

The heat from the fire was overwhelming, and Calista took a step back. She couldn't get over that Håkan had said he was lucky to find her. She nodded, trying to think of something to say.

"So how was it at your grandma's?" she asked again. "I haven't seen you in a while."

"It was sad," Håkan said. "My grandma has Alzheimer's, and Mom and I had to help her move into a nursing home. Still, it was good to spend time with her. She told me stories about when she was little that I didn't know."

Håkan and Calista slowly drifted away from the fire, making their way around the festive city. Soon, they found themselves on the lawn of Uppsala Cathedral, looking up at the dark red twin steeples stretching into the sky.

"This church is enormous," Calista said. "We went inside yesterday."

Håkan nodded. "Someone told me it's the tallest church in Scandinavia. Some famous people are buried in the crypts inside."

"Like who?" Calista asked.

"Like King Gustavus Vasa, and Saint Erik, the patron saint of Sweden, and the botanist Carl von Linné."

"We studied him in biology last year," Calista said. "He's the guy who named the plants and organized them into families, right?"

"The very same," Håkan said.

They walked quietly up and down the hills around the cathedral. Calista was getting tired, but she didn't want to go back to the dorms just yet. In fact, she didn't want this night ever to end. She was completely comfortable by Håkan's side.

"There's something I've wanted to ask you," Håkan said after a few moments of silence. "But I feel kind of stupid, because it's really none of my business."

"Go ahead," Calista said. "Ask away."

"Whatever happened to that boyfriend you had?"

"He dumped me," she said, a little too eagerly. "Months ago. In fact, I never even saw him after I arrived."

"Oh," Håkan said. "I figured it was over, since I never saw him around, but I wasn't sure."

The hopeful tone in his voice made Calista feel almost jittery with happiness. She chuckled. "Actually, I'm glad we broke up. I think I've had a better time here without him.

And I've learned a lot of things I don't think I would have learned if I'd still been going out with him."

Håkan was walking close to Calista, his hand occasionally brushing against hers. "Like what?" he asked.

Now *that* was a personal question, but she hesitated only for a moment. She felt safe with Håkan.

"Hm, how do I say this," she began self-consciously. "For one thing, I've learned that I haven't chosen boyfriends well, and often for the wrong reasons."

Håkan listened intently.

"I've tried pleasing other people, dating a guy because somebody else thought I should or because he was a great athlete and I knew my dad would like him. That's stupid, isn't it?"

"Not stupid," Håkan said. "Understandable. But it's good that you're recognizing it. Now you can make better choices." He smiled broadly at her.

Calista returned the smile. "It's late," she said tentatively. "I'd better get back. Lena might start worrying about me."

People were still singing and walking around town when Håkan and Calista approached the Studentstaden, but things were calming down. There was a general happy-tired feeling.

"Let's get together when we get back home," Håkan said when they reached Studentstaden. He looked at her, strangely, she thought, then smiled his warm smile. He reached out and gently pulled her into a hug, then said good-bye and turned to leave.

Calista watched him go. It was strange how good she felt when she was with Håkan. She thought about Suzanne and what Suzanne had said about Mike in her e-mails. Did Calista feel the same way about Håkan? How did she know that her infatuation with him wasn't just another example of her wanting to please someone? Lena had suggested they go see him at the game store that time. She seemed really to like Håkan, and would probably be pleased if he and Calista got together. Lena's happiness was important to her, but could that really be all there was to it? Maybe, but no matter how much she tried to shake it off, she couldn't help feeling that things with Håkan were different somehow. And different was a good thing, she hoped.

Chapter Nine

Back at Klara Norra all the classroom windows were open. It was three days after *Valborg* and the warm, sunny spring weather still held. The elm trees outside had turned green, and the lawns were bright with dandelions. Calista's thoughts kept returning to her walk with Håkan, and how his hand had brushed against hers. She pushed them away. It would be stupid to let herself fall for him now that she was going home in just a month. Besides, he hadn't called, and it was already Thursday.

Even though it was seventy degrees Fahrenheit outside, Ripan was wearing her standard dark blue woolen dress. "I hope you have all read the texts by Isaiah Berlin for today," she said. "Who wants to explain the concept of 'free will'?"

Calista bent over her notebook, pretending to take notes. It had seemed simple enough when Ripan explained it to them in class, but the texts they had read for today's homework were confusing. Free will didn't exactly mean doing what you wanted...more like—

Before Calista could stop it, her hand was in the air.

"Calista," Ripan said, nodding.

"Free will is the power to choose," Calista said. "Which could also mean that there is nobody to blame but our-selves in the end."

Ripan nodded and gave her a rare smile. "You've learned something this semester," she said. She turned around and started writing on the blackboard.

Hm, Calista thought. She knew she had free will. Nobody had really coerced her into dating someone she didn't want to date. She had chosen to defer to other people, not just about boys, but about a lot of things. She had let other people decide for her—so she didn't have to. She had been taking the easy way out. Was she still?

At the end of class, Calista was still thinking about it.

That evening, putting off her homework, Calista logged on to e-mail Leah and Sammie about it. At the last minute, she decided to send the e-mail to Suzanne as well.

Från: Calista@email.com

Till: Sammiesam@email.com, leahwinter@email.com, Suzic@email.com

Ämne: Håkan

I just had to write you guys. I guess I'm a little confused. I think it's because of this free will discussion we had in philosophy class today. I'm not sure what is *my* will, and what's other people's will anymore.

There's this guy, Håkan. I think I've told you all about him. He was in Uppsala when I was there, and he and I both got separated from the people we were with, and ended up spending part of the night together. He is amazing, and he said he wanted to see me again. I like him, but I'm not sure if it's because I think my friend Lena approves. How can you tell if your choices are really your own? Oh, and there is of course the issue of time—it's only a MONTH until I have to leave. What's the point of going out with the guy now, even if I figure out I want to? Anyway, I don't really want advice because I think I need to decide for myself for once. I just needed to vent. Miss you guys,

Cal

Britta brought Calista a cup of tea later that evening when she was struggling with her philosophy homework.

"Your Swedish is amazingly improved, Calista," Britta said after reading through the paragraph Calista had asked her to check for grammar errors. "I never thought you would speak and write this well at the end of only one semester."

"Don't remind me it's almost the end of the semester," Calista said accusingly. "I'm not done being here yet."

Britta leaned down to give her a hug. "We're not done having you, Calista. You'll have to come back again." She stood up brusquely. "It's much too early to talk like that, though. You have more than three weeks left."

The phone on her desk rang, and Calista picked it up.

"Håkan," she mouthed to Britta, her heart beating in her throat. Britta grinned and tiptoed out of the room.

"Do you want to come to Drottningholm's Castle with me on Saturday?" Håkan asked, after they'd exchanged hellos.

She hesitated. Yes, she wanted to! But no, she shouldn't! She wasn't sure how she really felt, and she was leaving soon, and...

"Um...I can't," she said finally, her voice thin, her mind searching frantically for an excuse. "I have to work on my Swedish culture project. I'm presenting on Monday and I still have to finish my Styrofoam model of a rune stone. I'm sorry. I'm sure it would be fun. I had a really nice time with you in Uppsala." She was babbling. This was so embarrassing. Then, before she could make a complete idiot of

herself, she blurted, "Well, thanks for calling. Talk to you soon!" She'd barely heard him mumble, "Oh, okay," before she hung up.

Oh, no, what had she done? Why couldn't things be simple and easy? What was it about this guy that turned her into a complete idiot? He called to ask her on a date, and she'd practically hung up on him.

She was in full panic mode now. Håkan was so wonderful, and she'd ruined everything just because she couldn't make a decision on her own. She started to dial Lena's number to ask for her advice, then stopped herself. Lena was a good friend, but she couldn't always turn to her friends for help with decisions. She knew she hadn't chosen perfect guys in the past, but there was something different about Håkan. There was something different about how she felt when she was with him. She felt like the best version of herself, she realized. When she was with him, they talked about things that interested her as much as him, and she didn't just sit by and let him walk all over her.

She took a deep breath. Her hand shook as she dialed Håkan's number, but she knew she was making the right decision. Luckily, he answered right away, before she had a chance to change her mind.

"Calista, hi," he said, sounding tentative.

"I *can* go on Saturday, after all," she said, willing her voice to work. She tried to think of an explanation as to why she'd said no before, but couldn't think of anything.

There was a brief pause before Håkan said, "Oh…um… great. I'll stop by your house at nine."

Calista grinned from ear to ear.

On Saturday morning, Håkan arrived at nine, exactly when he said he would. He parked his black Saab in front of the Öhströms' row house. He greeted Calista, and Bengt and Britta, and they all chatted for a few minutes before he and Calista took off. They had decided that morning on the phone that they would take the train so Håkan wouldn't have to worry about parking in the city. They'd be taking the boat from City Hall Bridge to the castle anyway, so they wouldn't need the car.

As they started walking through the residential area of Spånga, toward the commuter train station, they passed Moa's house. Moa hadn't said more than two words to Calista this whole semester, and Calista still wondered how Håkan could be so close to her.

"Now that I know you two aren't dating," Calista started cautiously, "I just wonder what has made you such good friends. Moa hasn't been too friendly to me, which makes me think she might have a crush on you or something."

"Trust me, Moa would rather die a slow, torturous death than go out with me," Håkan said. "It would be like dating her brother."

Håkan and Calista showed their passes at the booth for

the commuter train and got on the train. It was crowded for a Saturday morning. They had to stand and hold on to the bars attached to the ceiling of the train.

"Moa's and my family did things together when we were growing up." Håkan explained. "When I was ten, my dad left my mom for a twenty-five-year-old."

"I'm sorry," Calista said. "That must have been hard."

"It was hard at the time," Håkan said. "Now my dad and his new wife, Ann-Marie, have two little kids, and I'm okay with it. Anyway, Moa's family took care of me a lot when my mom worked."

The train shook, and Calista bumped into Håkan. He held his arm out to steady her.

"Six months ago, Moa's dad left her mom for a younger woman, an American actress, and they moved to Hollywood."

"Oh, the American connection."

"Yup, you got it. I think that's why she isn't exactly warm and fuzzy with you."

"Oh," Calista said. "That explains it." She felt bad for Moa, but she was relieved that Moa's distance had nothing to do with her liking Håkan.

The loudspeaker announced Stockholm Central. The train stopped, and they got off.

"Instead of taking the subway, let's walk to City Hall Bridge," Håkan said.

They climbed the stairs from the commuter train terminals into the central hall above them. Calista remembered the first time she had been here, her first day of school, when she had lost her way.

The city was full of people enjoying the warm weather. A horse pulling a cart of camera-wielding tourists trotted by as Calista and Håkan passed the tall Sheraton Hotel building, and turned right to cross the City Hall Bridge. From there, they could see Gamla Stan across the water in the distance, and, more closely, the enormous red-brick City Hall building, with its three golden crowns on top of the tall spire.

They strolled along the quay by City Hall, watching a flock of white swans fighting for the bread crumbs a little girl was throwing to them.

"Wow," Calista noted, "you can see a lot of churches from here." She pointed across the water to a beautiful church with two spiky spires, another one to the left of it, and yet another one to its right. "I'll miss all these beautiful sights when I go home," she said. "There isn't exactly a cityscape in Moon Lake."

"Your family must be excited about your coming back," Håkan said. "Do you miss them?"

"Sometimes," Calista said, thoughtfully. "I love being here, but I'm looking forward to spending more time with my twin sister, Suzanne."

They walked quietly, heading toward the City Hall Bridge again. Sailboats were crisscrossing the bay in front

of them, and seagulls were screaming above. "Suzanne and I were really close when we were little," Calista said. "Then, in junior high, we started growing apart somehow. Since I've been here, I've learned not to take my relationship with her for granted. Now I can't wait to get to know her again. Though," she added, "I'm *not* in a hurry to leave Sweden."

Håkan nodded. "There's the steamboat," he said, pointing.

Calista had expected the steamboat to be old and rickety, but this one was shiny white, and looked brand-new.

As soon as the woman in charge had pulled the rope aside, Håkan and Calista hopped on board and made their way to the top deck.

There couldn't be a city in the world more beautiful than Stockholm, Calista thought as the boat started out toward the middle of the channel, making its way through the city. The sun was glinting off the water, adding an almost magical sparkle to all the buildings and people.

Soon they left the traffic and most of the large city buildings behind. Cabins edged the lake around them. A voice on a loudspeaker announced the names of the islands they passed: Rotholmen, Björnholmen, Tallholmen.

"That island looks uninhabited," Calista said, pointing. "Or is it even an island?"

"It is," Håkan answered. "It's called Kärsön. Every kid

in Stockholm goes there at some point during his middle school years to walk in nature, swim, and have outdoor picnics. It's beautiful, and they have great sports facilities."

The boat had rounded the tip of Kärsön and was approaching another large island, Lovön. An enormous sparkling, cream-colored castle came into view. It was stately and elegant, and like a fairy tale in its beauty.

"Now *this* is a palace," Calista burst out. "Much fancier than the square one downtown."

Håkan laughed. "I knew you'd like it. The royal family's lived here since 1981. The first Royal Palace was actually built here in the 1500s by King Johan III, but it burned down. They started building this one sometime in the late 1600s."

"Wow, that's old. How do you know?"

"You're not supposed to ask, just be impressed with how knowledgeable I am," Håkan joked.

Calista shoved him gently with her elbow. "So how *do* you know?"

"Okay." He laughed. "I looked it up so I could impress you."

"I *am* impressed. I'm *really* impressed."

The boat landed at the dock behind the castle.

"We have a few different options," Håkan said. "We could go into the castle, but it's not that exciting, since you don't get to see the part where the royal family lives.

Another option is to walk through the parks, and then end up at the Chinese Pavilion, which is really cool, and which I happen to know a lot about." Håkan winked.

Calista laughed and followed Håkan onto the gangway.

"Let's do the parks and the Chinese Pavilion," she said.

They walked around to the other side of the castle, where a magnificent park spread out in front of them. A cluster of fountains sprayed water in dancing patterns. On both sides of the fountains were symmetrical gardens, immaculately raked gravel paths, and bushes so well trimmed not a leaf appeared to be out of place.

"This is really something," Calista said. "Can you imagine being the gardener here? It's beautiful, but almost too structured."

"I agree," Håkan said. "This garden is French Baroque, made in the style of the Versailles gardens outside of Paris. You'll like the English gardens better. I do."

"What's that?" Calista asked, pointing away from the castle to what looked like a tall, thick, green hedge, immaculately trimmed to look like a wall.

"Oh, that..." Håkan said, a devilish grin on his face. "I'll show you." He started jogging toward the hedge, and before Calista knew it, he disappeared into it. As she got closer, she noticed a concealed opening in the wall of green.

Calista walked through the opening. Inside, she followed a path, winding this way and that, then stopping abruptly. She backtracked, found another path, then a dead end. It was a labyrinth, she realized, an enormous hedge labyrinth. On the other side of the hedge the gravel rustled. Calista stopped in her tracks. She held her breath. Håkan was trying to find her in the labyrinth, but she would find him first. She tiptoed through the narrow passage. At another dead end, she backed up, trying to figure out the way she had come in. But now she was too deep into the labyrinth. She heard the gravel again and stood still, an odd tingling sensation in her stomach. She turned around the bend. She was in a small, green courtyard, just large enough for a wooden bench in the center. She still couldn't see Håkan, but she heard him breathing. She grinned. She'd get him.

But before Calista realized what was happening, Håkan stepped out from a shielded place in the hedge behind her. Gently, he placed his hands on her shoulders and turned her around, his brown eyes looking right into hers. He was smiling. Then, so slowly it felt as though time had stopped, he put his hand on the back of her head, leaned into her, and covered her lips with his.

Calista held her breath. Thoughts were coursing through her mind. No. Yes. Stop. Don't stop. Her hands went to Håkan's chin. She touched the stubble, then let her fingers move to caress his hair. This is what she'd wanted to do

ever since she first saw him, she realized. She closed her eyes and forgot about everything but Håkan.

"Remember when you opened the door at the Öhströms' house on New Year's Eve?" Håkan mumbled after an eternity, pulling his face a few inches away from hers.

"I remember," Calista said dreamily.

They walked, their arms around each other, to the small wooden bench and sat down.

"You looked so hopeful and welcoming. You were the cutest thing I'd ever seen. You looked like you were bursting with excitement. When Moa made that comment about your boyfriend, I was so disappointed."

"What took you so long to kiss me, then?" Calista said, gently teasing. "You found out that it was over with Jonas when we were in Uppsala. You could have kissed me then."

"Maybe," Håkan said, "but you're not that easy to read. When I held you by the bonfire, you seemed almost afraid of me."

Calista stood and pulled Håkan up. "I was just a little unsure," she said. "But I'm not anymore." She smiled. "Let's go see the other gardens, and while we walk, I'll tell you about Calista, the very confused exchange student."

As they walked, Calista poured out her life story. When she finished telling Håkan about it, Håkan pulled her to him again. He held her for a long time, until Calista felt their breathing synchronize. He kissed her again, then laced his fingers through hers and continued walking.

As Håkan had promised, Calista liked the English garden much more than the French. But maybe this was because Håkan kept encircling her with his arms, and holding her underneath the centuries-old oak trees every few steps.

They took their time exploring the rest of the gardens and the Chinese Pavilion, and eventually they made their way to a café for lunch, and then back to the train station. By the end of the afternoon, Calista was sure it had been the most amazing day she'd experienced in Sweden thus far. It wasn't just that the castle and grounds were beautiful, or even that she and Håkan had spent most of the day with their arms entwined, it was that she finally felt like she had done exactly what she wanted to do, exactly when she wanted to do it, without worrying about what anyone else thought. She had chosen to spend time with Håkan, no matter what her friends, or Suzanne, or Moa, or anyone else thought. And, judging by the warm feeling inside that lingered even after Håkan had left, she had chosen well.

Från: Suzic@email.com
Till: Calista@email.com
Ämne: Stuff

Cal, because you said you didn't want advice about Håkan, I'm not going to give you any. And I don't think you

need it. I'm sure you can figure out what you want. (But I *am* curious to see how it went, so could you at least tell me?)

Guess what? I'm gonna take a year off from piano. I've really liked not playing for a while. I know I'll want to play again, but I need a break to figure things out. And guess what else? I've decided to study abroad in college. Your adventure in Sweden has made me realize I want to do something exciting, too. I still have to figure out where I want to go though.

You know how I was looking forward to your coming home so you could see Mike? Well, now I'm mostly just looking forward to your coming home so I can see *you*. I think we've both changed since you left, and it'll be fun to be sisters again. I feel like we haven't been for a while. I've missed you.

Love ya,
Suze

Från: Calista@email.com
Till: Suzic@email.com
Ämne: Study abroad

Suze,

I *did* go out with Håkan. We went to Drottningholms Castle and…he kissed me. It's difficult to think about anything else right now. I'm starting to understand how you

186

feel about Mike. This is so not how it was with Jonas. Yes, I talked about him a lot, but it didn't really have to do with my feelings for him as much as the fact that he was my boyfriend and that was a cool thing. This is hard for me to explain, but I think you understand. I hate the thought of leaving Håkan now that I am getting close to him. I know I'll see him again, though.

I feel like you, Suze, like we had lost the sister thing but that we're getting it back. I miss you, too.

There's so much I want to talk to you about....

XXOO

Cal

Chapter Ten

"Initially, I wanted to learn about the Vikings because of the runes," Calista said as she began her presentation in Swedish culture class on Monday afternoon. Several other classes had been invited to the presentations, and it was crowded and hot in the room.

"However, I quickly learned three important facts that expanded my viewpoint," she continued. "One—there is no such thing as a Viking, at least not what we have in mind when we talk about Vikings. Two—people before and after the time we think of as the Viking era also used runes. But most important, three—there is so much more to this time period in Swedish history than rune stones and fighting and pillaging."

Calista brought out her first prop from the closet in the front of the classroom—the almost life-sized Styrofoam rune stone that she had spray-painted gray and on which she had carved a slithering snake; inside the snake she had engraved a rune message. She propped the stone up against the wall where the students could see it.

"Since the runes were my main reason for choosing this era, though, I will begin with the rune stones," she said as she began handing out a rune alphabet with a code on how to translate the runes.

"As you can see," she said, "several of the runes stand for any number of modern-day letters, which makes it tricky to interpret the message, even when it's very simple, like this one. It says, 'Here lies Björn. Slain in the east. The stone was raised by Torulf, his brother.'"

Calista turned from the rune stone. "I think these stones were appealing to me in part because of my interest in the Swedish language—old and new. I wanted to come to Sweden to learn to speak Swedish, and when I arrived, I realized there was so much more to learn and to appreciate about Sweden than just the language," she said. The other foreign students nodded.

"The assumptions I had about the Vikings were the same ones I had about Swedes in general. In my mind, Swedes were a homogeneous group of people, all of

whom looked, if not exactly the same, at least similar. Over this semester I have found that Swedes, and Vikings, don't let themselves be categorized that easily. There is no way to lump the peoples together. Most people from the Viking era, it turns out, were not seafaring pirates, but peaceful farmers and artisans."

Calista continued her presentation, showing photos from the Royal Mounds of Gamla Uppsala and the rune stones in Grödinge. She brought out a small clay replica she had made of the Royal Mounds, and a model of a tiny longhouse, the dwelling some Viking-era people lived in, which she had bought in the Historical Museum gift shop.

She found that the more enthusiasm she felt for her subject, the more spellbound her audience seemed to be. She talked about how the pagan religion, with its worship of Odin and Thor, and many other Nordic gods during the Viking era, reflected the lifestyle of the times. Then the introduction of Christianity, she told her audience, changed the power structure in the villages, eventually leading to the demise of the peoples called "Vikings."

At the conclusion of the presentations, as everyone filed out of the classroom, Calista noticed that Moa had been standing in the back of the room. She caught Moa's eye. Moa did her little chin lift but, somehow, today it didn't feel dismissive. Maybe it was just how she communicated, Calista thought. Maybe it didn't have anything to do with her. Maybe it had never had anything to do with her.

Kathy motioned for Calista to come over. As Calista got close, she saw the small piece of paper Kathy held up. It had only three letters on it, MBG—*Med beröm godkänt*—Pass with distinction.

The following Saturday, Calista was strangely excited about spending a day by herself, snapping photos all over Stockholm. She fiddled with her camera as the train rattled into the tunnel before Gamla Stan. Calista could see the tunnel walls through the windows, and, in the dark, a reflection of her own face. Her hair had grown longer since she came to Sweden. She wondered how long Suzanne's hair was now. Maybe they would look alike again when she got home. For the first time in years, the thought didn't bother her. She wanted them to be twins again. It was even difficult to remember why she had been so eager to distance herself from her sister. For some reason, Suzanne's piano playing had made her feel so inferior. In Sweden, she had found that she had her own strengths, and that they had nothing to do with dating the right guy or pleasing other people.

The subway slowed, and Calista stood up.

She stepped off the train. Huge H&M billboards covered the walls on the other side of the tracks. Calista noticed she was wearing the same shirt as one of the models in the picture.

From the subway station, Calista walked Munkbroleden along the water, following the sidewalk in front of the centuries-old apartment buildings. On the other side of the water she could see Slussen, the lock between Lake Mälaren and the Baltic Sea, and beyond that, Katarinahissen, the elevator connecting this part of town with Mosebacke, on top of the hill.

She snapped pictures as she went. Unwilling to leave the water view, she continued all the way to the end of Gamla Stan and turned left when she reached the bridges leading to Södermalm. She walked the narrow alley up to Järntorget and, from there, headed toward the center of the island.

Continuing to snap pictures, Calista strolled toward her favorite coffee shop in Stortorget. She loved the ornate buildings surrounding Stortorget. The five-story struc-ture in which the coffee shop was housed was painted a beautiful medieval-looking rusty red. Calista entered café Kaffekoppen and grabbed coffee and a pastry.

After eating her snack, she spent the rest of the day strolling around Stockholm, filling her digital camera's memory card with images of the city. She watched the changing of the guard at the Royal Palace, people-watched on a park bench in Kungsträdgården, and walked barefoot through the fountain in the middle of the garden.

It was growing dark when she finally made her way

back to the commuter train, trying to savor every last moment of her sightseeing.

As she neared the train station, a young Swedish couple passed her. The guy strode confidently, his arm around the girl's waist, her body leaning into his in an intimate way. Something about the guy's high-held head and cocky walk reminded Calista of Jonas. She realized that, had things been different, she might have been walking the streets of Stockholm with him today. It amazed her that she had arrived just a few months ago with one set of expectations, only to have something totally different unfold. While Jonas had turned out to be a jerk, he did prompt her to take some time out for herself. And now she knew she could walk through Stockholm, or anywhere for that matter, by herself without feeling scared and lonely. Sometime during her semester abroad she had discovered that she was a different person—a stronger person—than she had thought.

The last day of school, the day before Calista departed for Wisconsin, started out gray and rainy, but before the commuter train reached Stockholm Central, the sun pushed its way through the clouds, and the world outside was glittering with newly fallen rain.

It felt strange to Calista knowing she would never walk this route again. She was starting to feel just the tiniest

twinge of excitement when thinking about going home to see her parents and Suzanne, and Leah and Sammie. Still, the thought of saying good-bye to the people and places she had come to love was overwhelming.

By the time Calista arrived, the auditorium at Klara Norra was filled to the last seat for the graduation assembly. As always when she had time to reflect on it, Calista was awestruck with the sense of history of the building that housed Klara Norra Gymnasium. A hundred years ago students had sat here like she did now, listening to the principal's long-winded speech (it wouldn't surprise her if it was the same principal). A small heart scratched into the wooden pew in front of her might have been carved by someone who lived during World War I.

Like Calista, nobody seemed to be listening to the principal. Not even Lena, who usually paid attention to teachers. She was writing a text message to Mark on her cell phone. Calista felt an annoying itching in her eyes. She'd known it for a long time, but it was really starting to hit home how hard it would be to leave Lena.

Her thoughts were interrupted by an enormous roar. Suddenly, white graduation hats were flying around her. "Next year, it's my turn," Lena called beside Calista, trying to make herself heard above the din. "And after I graduate, I'm coming to see you."

Calista turned to Lena to give her a hug. This time her eyes didn't just itch. They flooded over with tears.

Outside in the school yard, behind a thick crowd of parents, siblings, relatives, and friends of the graduates, stood two dray horses in front of an enormous wagon furnished with hay bales and decorated with birch branches, lilacs, and tiny Swedish flags.

Monique stepped out of the crowd and took hold of Calista's arm. "Hey, Calista," she hollered, "grab Lena and get on. This wagon is for Marie. She said you guys should come."

Calista pulled at Lena's arm. "Come on," she called.

She and Lena clambered up onto the wagon just in time before it started moving. To Calista's surprise, the students started singing.

"Sing about the happy days of a student," they sang at the top of their voices, many of them crying, waving bouquets in the air. "Let us be joyful in the spring of our youth. Our hearts are still beating happily, and the dawning future is ours."

From the north, on Kungsgatan, another hay cart full of singing students approached. Calista hadn't thought it possible, but the students on both carts managed to sing even louder as they got closer, waving at one another and jumping up and down.

"This makes our American graduation seem so boring," Calista yelled in Lena's ear. "I love it."

Hours later, the wagon full of students arrived back at Klara Norra's school yard. Calista was hoarse from all

the shouting and singing, and dizzy with the craziness of Swedish graduation.

She hugged Monique hard when she jumped off. Monique, too, was returning to the States the following day. "Don't cry," Monique said with a wink as they were saying good-bye. "We might see each other sooner than you think."

What does that mean? Calista wondered, but she gave Monique another hug and turned away. She hated good-byes.

"I'm coming with you for supper," Lena said as they started toward the train through the mass of white-hatted students with flower wreaths around their necks.

"Great!" Calista said. "I'm sure that's fine with Britta." She was relieved that she wouldn't have to say good-bye to Lena just yet.

"It is. She already knows," Lena said.

Indeed, Britta and Bengt did know. When Lena and Calista arrived, a huge *smörgåsbord* filled the dining room table. There was herring, lox with sprigs of dill, tiny Swedish meatballs, newly baked cumin loaves, tiny little hot dogs, cheeses, pickled beets, liverwurst, *Janssons frestelse*, a potato au gratin with anchovies, boiled and deviled eggs, and much more. There were also desserts of lingonberry mousse, pear tarts, and fruit salad.

Lena and Calista barely had a chance to take their

coats and shoes off before the house started filling up with people. Most of Bengt and Britta's friends were there, including Moa and Karin, as well as many of the people who had attended the New Year's party. Aunt Pernilla brought a tiny, red, hand-painted horse from the Dalarna region of western Sweden for Calista, and she kept complimenting Calista on her Swedish.

To Calista's surprise, Monique was there, too. She had escaped from Marie's graduation party for a few hours.

"That's what you meant by seeing me sooner than I might think," Calista said.

"I couldn't give away the surprise, could I?"

Calista laughed. Everyone must be here now, she thought, but the doorbell rang again. "You get it," Britta said to her.

It was Håkan.

"Hey, I thought you were working at Radio Stockholm until seven tonight," she said, happy in his warm embrace.

"I made that up so you wouldn't know about the party," he said. "I'll work more shifts after you leave. I'll be sad and will need something to do." He laughed as though he was joking, but Calista could see in his eyes that it was true. He would miss her.

Håkan leaned closer and whispered, "Britta's making sure the party lasts only until seven so you and I will have some time together, too."

Once again, Calista was stunned by Britta's thoughtfulness. When had she planned this entire party, and how did she always seem to know exactly what Calista needed?

When everyone had filled and refilled their plates from the *smörgåsbord* and had had a chance to eat and chat, Bengt, who never missed an opportunity to speak, stood up in the middle of the living room and clinked his glass.

He began, "On New Year's Eve, Britta and I told everyone how excited we were to have Calista for the semester. Now that the semester is over, we are starting to wonder if it was worth it."

Where was he going with this? Calista wondered. It made her a little nervous.

"What has happened," Bengt said, "is that we have come to care a great deal for our Cal, who works hard at everything she does, and who has been relentless in teaching herself Swedish and taking every learning opportunity offered. It is really, really hard to think about her going home. In fact, it is so hard that you have to wonder if having her here was worth the pain of her leaving."

Calista took a deep sigh. No, no, she thought. Don't do this, Bengt. Now she would cry in front of all these people.

Then Bengt laughed, though his eyes were shining. "Don't worry, Cal. Of course it's worth it—it's always worth allowing yourself to love someone. You'll just have to come back and visit us again soon."

"That's right," Håkan whispered behind her.

No more tears, Calista thought as she hugged Britta. But it was too late, they were streaming down her cheeks. "I'll miss you and Bengt so much," she said, sniffling. Britta wiped her eyes.

"We'll miss you, too, sweetie," she said.

"Can I cry now?" Calista asked when she hugged Monique good-bye for the second time that day. "Yes, now you can cry," Monique said, her own mascara running down her cheeks.

"Will you miss Jens?" Calista asked.

Monique grinned at Calista. "Jens who?" Then she added, still smiling, "I'm kidding, Calista, I'm not as bad as you think. Of course I'll miss Jens. He's the best thing that happened to me in Sweden."

Calista looked at Monique, serious for once. "Monique, I don't think you're bad. You're as good as they come." She hugged her one more time before Monique walked out the door.

Lena waited until most of the other guests were gone before bringing her backpack out. "I've got something for you, Calista," she said, pulling a packet from her bag.

Calista eagerly started unwrapping the thin tissue paper around the packet. It wasn't...It couldn't be...

"Oh my God, Lena," she said, holding the black-, red-, and gold-colored wall hanging for Bengt and Britta to see.

"Where did you get that, Lena?" Britta said. "It's exquisite. I've never seen anything like it."

Lena laughed. "It took Calista coming all the way from America to tell me that I'm an artist and that I should take it seriously. My stepdad has been telling me for years, but somehow I managed to ignore him. Then Calista came and made a big fuss about the stuff I made."

"You *made* it!" Bengt said.

Lena nodded. "I've only let my family hang my artwork at our cabin, but the thought of Calista having my art somewhere in her house in America, even if she puts it in a closet, is kind of exciting. It'll be like a little piece of me with her in Moon Lake."

"A closet?" Calista laughed. "You must be kidding. This one's going in the living room. I'll even put a museum-quality placard underneath it. What's it called?"

"Study Abroad," Lena said, "though I didn't know it when I made it."

Study Abroad, Calista thought. How appropriate. There was the beautiful, shiny black cloth on the outside, alluring, yet a little frightening. Through the rips and tears in the dark fabric, you could see the red and the gold fabrics shining through, like all the joyful experiences she had had in Sweden, some of them because of a rip or a tear…or a breakup.

"Saying good-bye to you is hard, Lena," Calista said, setting the wall hanging down on the table.

Lena smiled, but she, too, had tears running down her cheeks when she hugged Calista and stepped out the door. "Remember, I'm coming after I graduate. It's only a year."

"Good," Calista said. "Then I won't say good-bye. I'll just say see you later."

Lena smiled. "See you later," she said.

Håkan waited until after Lena had left to give Calista a strong hug, taking away some of the pain of the good-bye. "Let's go for a walk," he said.

Håkan and Calista followed the sidewalk between the row houses until they hit the gravel path taking them into the park behind the buildings. All the leaves were finally out on the trees, and from people's gardens came the sweet smell of early summer flowers. From the porches lining the park Calista could hear scattered noises of graduation parties.

"I've never met anyone like you, Cal," Håkan said when they reached a stand of maples. He stopped and held her face in his hands, looking serious. "So...hungry for life. I hate that you're going home now that I'm just getting to know you."

Calista leaned into him and kissed him gently. "I know exactly what you mean," she said. Because at the same time that Håkan was getting to know her, Calista had been getting to know herself. And, though she hated the thought that tomorrow she'd be on a plane, leaving Håkan

and Sweden and everything she'd come to love, she knew that her adventure would not be forgotten. Whatever the future held, whatever decisions she made for herself, and wherever she went, she would carry Sweden inside her forever.

Turn the page for a special preview of another

novel:

Girl Overboard

Chapter One

Marina cringed as her monstrous purple suitcase slid down the baggage ramp and landed with a sickening thud on top of a small carry-on. A matching petite girl standing next to Marina wailed in dismay.

As the travelers crowding the baggage claim in Miami International struggled to help free the girl's little mushed bag from under the purple hulk, Marina Gray surveyed the situation and decided to sit tight and let her mother's idea of stylish luggage make a second round of the corral.

One perk of being several thousand miles south of her Vermont hometown was that no one knew her name. This

happened to be a good thing since "Marina" was engraved along with three jumping dolphins on the silver handle of the embarrassing bag. As it came back around, she took a deep breath and hauled the suitcase up.

Standing on tiptoe, she tried to locate the Students Across the Seven Seas contact person, but Miami International was packed with people dressed in gaudy fluorescent sundresses and Hawaiian shirts. March in Vermont was still three-feet-of-snow-on-the-ground freezing. But her plane mates had scattered, leaving her a lone stretch-cord-jeans-and-boots fish in a sea of flip-flops.

"Fish out of water," she mumbled. "Great, I've officially become a cliché."

A group of tourists in matching "his and her" hot pink shirts and muumuus surrounded her and she felt the sudden, uncomfortable sensation of being hijacked by a flock of overweight flamingos. She rose on her toes again. For once, she was grateful for her five foot eleven inches as she spotted a man in a bright orange S.A.S.S. polo. She pushed up her long sleeves and picked her way through the crowd, almost panting from the effort.

"Marina?" asked a deep voice through the whitest smile she had ever seen.

The guy was right out of the fashion mags: jet black hair, tanned skin, broad shoulders—he was even tall.

Marina dragged her eyes away from him and tried not

to blush. He reached for her suitcase and she almost forgot to let go of the handle. With a second tug and a smile, he pulled it up and put it on the trolley covering two nearly identical streamlined black backpacks.

"Did you know that your mouth is hanging open?" said a heavily accented French girl standing beside the S.A.S.S. advisor. Her glossy dark hair was pulled back into a casual twist that looked like it took two seconds to put up. Marina had tried the look once, but only ended up with cramped arms and a mess of long, blonde tangles. She had stuck to braids after that.

The thin blonde next to the French girl snickered at the obvious comment. Marina snapped her mouth shut and gave up the useless fight not to blush. She stared at her boots instead.

"Er, how did you know I'm Marina?" she stammered at the ground.

"Well, unless you answer to Lincoln and are a white-water raft guide from Australia, you'd pretty much have to be Marina." He smiled.

"Right. Then, yes, I would be Marina." She attempted a smile back.

Marina had spent the plane trip convincing herself it was okay to leave the old version of herself behind. After so many years coasting, knowing everyone in her tiny town and them knowing her, it was time to start fresh. She could do first impressions. No problem. She pulled herself up and

smiled again with confidence. "What's your name?" Marina asked as he handed her his clipboard to sign.

"Marco. I'm the program advisor, and also one of the instructors."

She looked up and stared. One dimple. The guy had one dimple. It was simply too much. That one dimple doomed her to a whole new kind of cliché—crush-on-the-teacher cliché. The worst.

"Oh. 'Marco' is Spanish, right?" she asked with some effort.

"Italiano, actually," Marco said.

"Not everyone in Miami is Hispanic you know," said the other girl in a thick Southern drawl.

The two girls sidled up to each other. One nudged the other and murmured something at which they both giggled. These two were going to be trouble, Marina could tell already.

"Well, half-Italian. Half-Dominican. My mother's from the Dominican Republic," he added with a wink for Marina.

At the wink, Marina felt one knee buckle. Not both knees, just one. This was good; she could control a one-knee-buckling crush. And a nice, harmless crush on an instructor—a very young instructor—could distract her from dwelling on her boyfriend, Damon, the whole time.

She and Damon had been inseparable for three years. Their friends had even given them the annoying nickname "Damarina." She loved Damon, but tended to be of the

4

opinion that a girl deserved her own name. And Damon had not been pleased at this latest escapade of hers. "Why do you have to go away to figure us out?" he had asked. Breaking the news that she was going to be studying abroad on a six-week program at sea, and why, had not been easy.

There were the obvious reasons. She had been nearly obsessed with dolphins and all sea life since going to Sea World when she was eight. She had been the audience participant during the show, and the minute the dolphin snatched the little fish from her hand, something clicked. Even her name—what could "Marina" mean but that she was destined to become a marine biologist?

Dreaming of becoming the next Jackie Cousteau was not very practical in Vermont, but Marina did what she could. She volunteered at the Northern Vermont Fish Hatchery to soak up knowledge from the biologists about fish and sea life. She spent idle hours just sitting, digging her toes in the chilly sand and staring at massive Lake Champlain, which was hardly the sea, but a landlocked girl had to make do with what she could get. So when she saw the S.A.S.S. sign for the Caribbean Study Adventure with a marine biology focus and stops in the Bahamas, Utila, and the Dominican Republic, it was a no-brainer.

But this was Damon, her best friend and near constant companion since freshman year. He knew all of those things, but would look right through them and see the

doubt in her eyes. Things had been rocky between them lately. So besides the whole once-in-a-lifetime-amazing-tropical-experience reason for going, what could she say without seeming like a horrible person: I'm sorry your mom got sick, and I know why you want to stay in Vermont; but I need to figure out if I'm okay with your family situation changing our plans? I need to find out which is more awful—going away without you, or staying with you but stuck in this small town forever? I can't even tell if I still love you or if we rely on each other so much that you've become my safety net to help me make it in the world?

Scratch that last one. That one's way too scary. After all, that particular safety net had puppy dog brown eyes that crinkled when he smiled and wore her favorite cologne even though he hated it and…uh-oh. The beautiful Dominican/Italian teacher had been talking to her while she was lost in her imaginary conversation with her boyfriend.

"—is Natalia from Louisiana and Rheanna from France, both also with the S.A.S.S. program. Lincoln is joining us through another organization."

They all turned to survey the crowd, trying to pick out someone who looked like an Australian "Lincoln." Maybe he'd be wearing a safari hat with one side of the brim folded up.

As she watched the masses of tromping cruise-goers following a sombrero'ed Fiesta Line representative, she was glad she'd be on a boat with only fifteen other students and crew instead of three thousand like some of the ships boasted. The sleek lines and tinted windows of the *Tiburon* in her brochure looked more like it housed the champagne-and-caviar set than the all-you-can-eat-twenty-four-seven set.

Marina eyed the two girls standing next to her with suspicion. They were wearing almost identical black capris with white strappy tanks and sandals. When she looked closer, the blonde girl's pants looked like they had started out long and were just rolled up. Her tank also had a little insignia that said Miami, as if she bought it at the airport gift shop. Did Marina miss a memo about a required uniform? Maybe they were Stepford students. That whole "pulled together" look was so impossible for Marina, she couldn't even manage to work up a proper bit of jealousy over it.

She could feel a line of sweat trickling down her back and was thankful that her mom had pounced on her half-way through security and at least grabbed her winter coat. It was quite the scene though, her mom being detained by security for attempting to walk through the checkpoint without a boarding pass. That might have even made the *Woodchuck Post*, possibly costing her father the votes of all three readers, which would not have pleased his political cronies.

She checked out the girls again and stifled a giggle as they compared their matching giant movie star sunglasses.

These were S.A.S.S. girls though, so they had to be alright. The screening process was pretty comprehensive, both social and educational aspects were covered. Maybe she misread their attitude, different cultures or something. She'd never been to the South other than the one trip to Florida when she was little. She held out her hand and tried again.

"Hi, I'm Marina."

"Rhee."

"Tali."

Tali imitated Rhee's bored tone. They proceeded to ignore her, craning their necks trying to spot Lincoln. Rhee actually reached out and grabbed Marina's arm, moving her to one side to get a better look for the new arrival. Marina bristled. She was deciding how to respond when she saw Tali's eyes widen and heard her gasp. She spun around to see a vision in surf shorts heading their way.

Out of the crowd sauntered a buff, shaggy-haired guy. Glancing around, his eyes fell on Marco and then instantly slid to the three girls. He smiled a lazy smile. The girls were frozen in place. Marina was the first to break.

"No way," she breathed, grateful Damon wasn't there to see her new boatmate.

"WAY!" yelped Tali.

Rhee's long fingernails dug into Marina's upper arm. Marina pried them loose and flinched at Rhee's hiss.

"Le mien!"

She didn't need French 101 to understand a girl staking her claim on a guy. "Catty" was a universal language.

Marina looked from Marco to the stranger now signing the clipboard and shook her head. She wondered if maybe every place outside of Vermont was full of guys who could pose for Abercrombie ads. She certainly didn't care much about fashion and neither did her friends. For a state that spent half the year in knit hats, often complete with earflaps, the world of hair gel would forever remain a mystery and she was okay with that. Maybe this was just what the rest of the world looked like.

"Lincoln here, call me Link."

Boom, there went the other knee. That Aussie accent. He lightly tossed his huge duffel onto the baggage trolley and turned to the girls.

"G'day, sheilas!"

Marina's giggle ended in a small snort. *Arggh.* This always happened when she was nervous. She hoped others found it an endearing quality. Her mom assured her they did. But then again, her mom also claimed that she only knitted Marina's impractical but cute bikini tops triple thick to use up some extra yarn. In these matters, mothers weren't always the best ones to believe.

Link was looking straight into Marina's eyes with his head cocked. At least he wasn't taller than her, just exactly even. Maybe she would make it out of this airport without a wheelchair yet. They better not be picking up any other

guys, though. She was entirely kneeless as it was.

"Sorry, I didn't mean to laugh. I'm Marina. It's just, well, do you really talk like that?" she asked.

Link stepped close, invading her personal space. Marina tried to feel invaded, but failed. He reached out to play with the blonde wisps at the end of her thick braid.

"Marina," he whispered to himself.

He tossed her braid back over her shoulder and flashed a mischievous smile. "Look more like a Barbie to me."

He had already moved on to appraise the other girls and try as she might, Marina couldn't hold in her lifelong habit of making bad puns.

"Suppose you'll be throwing another shrimp on me, then."

Link paused mid-flirt with Rhee, who did not look pleased at the interruption, and laughed.

"Oh, this is gonna be a good trip." He caught her eye with a nod…and winked.